DESTINARE

A NOVEL

Matt Micros

"The only person you are destined to become is the person you decide to be."

Ralph Waldo Emerson

Also by Matt Micros

~*Five Days*~

~*The Knights of Redemption*~

~*The Chameleon*~

~*The Greatest Mann in the World*~

~*Nick Nelson Was Here*~

~*The Music Box*~

TABLE OF CONTENTS

DESTINARE

For shooting stars and ships that pass in the night...

I THE DECISION

*J*oe Moretti never wavered from the steely, intense expression on his face, not even after he heard the word *Cancer*. It was a word that left most people feeling as though they had been kicked in the guts by a steel-toed boot, and one that was powerful enough to reduce even the strongest of people to puddles of tears. But Joe wasn't wired that way. In the ten seconds since he had been informed of the diagnosis, he had already moved past the fear and anger and was already calculating survival percentages and wondering if, in poker terms, he was already pot committed enough in life to continue to fight for his survival.

"What are my chances?" Joe asked.

"Not good," the doctor answered. "I'm really sorry."

"Not good as in the chances of me being the starting point guard for the Knicks at age 44? Or not good as in my chances of winning Powerball tomorrow night?"

"Not good as in the chances of you surviving jumping out of an airplane at 30,000 feet without a parachute."

"Jesus. Don't sugar coat it, Doc. Give it to me straight."

The normally dry doctor chuckled at Joe's glib response. "I wish I had better news." At a time when many doctors had seen enough sickness and death to become immune to it, he actually seemed sincere.

"How long do I have?"

"With treatment? Maybe a couple of years."

"And without?"

"You'd be lucky to see ten months."

"Why wouldn't you have treatment?!!" his exasperated wife interjected. Leeanne was beautiful in a wholesome, girl next door sort of way, with a personality that lit up any room she entered which elevated her on the sexiness scale to off the chart sexy.

Joe carried forward as if she hadn't spoken, but it was clear he had heard her. He just preferred to have the doctor answer her question for him. "And how will I feel if I get treatment?"

"You'll be weak most days. Feel terribly some. Every now and then you'll have a good week."

"And if I don't get treatment?"

"You'll probably feel much as you do now, maybe even a little better if we give you some medicine to mask any pain. Until it turns..."

"And when do you think that would be?"

"There's no way of knowing. Could be a few months. Could be longer. But when it turns, it will be quick. We're talking weeks or less."

Joe nodded his head as if he had already made up his mind.

"You don't have to decide this minute," the doctor said, "Take a few days to think it over and discuss it with each other. If you have any questions, here's my cell number. Don't hesitate to use it."

A doctor's cell number was more coveted by people than a Maserati Granturismo. Too bad one had to be dying to get it.

~

"Don't you want to have as many days with me as possible?" Leeanne wailed once they had exited through the sliding doors of the hospital.

"Of course I do, but even more than that, I don't want to be a burden to you," he answered.

"You would never be a burden."

"You say that now, but I remember what it was like for my mother towards the end of my father's life. And I want to be remembered as the smart, funny, life of the party guy. Not as some broken-down, angry, bitter dying man."

"You'll be remembered as the life of the party guy, trust me."

"I'm not so sure. When I think back to my dad, I have to really strain to remember what he was like when he was younger and full of life."

"But you remember it."

"Yeah."

"And everyone will remember you the way you want them to. But can we not talk about this as if it's over? You could fight this and you could beat it."

"You heard the doctor, Lee. All that's left to do, is figure out how I want to go out. I really wish Phil Halmer was around. He would know what to do."

"Who's Phil Halmer? And why would he know?"

"He was my best friend in high school. Everyone loved him."

"I'm sure they loved you too."

"I'm serious. If you asked ten people about me, five might like me, three would hate me, and two would be indifferent."

"But you still haven't explained why he would know what to do?"

"Because Phil had failing kidneys and wasn't eligible for a transplant because of other health issues, so he went on dialysis."

"And what happened to him?"

"We lost touch over the years, but last I heard, he had decided to take himself off of dialysis, because his quality of life had deteriorated so much and because he was tired of being a burden on other people."

"So what happened to him?" Leeanne pressed.

"Truthfully, I don't know. He changed his number and disappeared. I don't think he wanted his friends to see him like that. And I think he knew I would have tried to talk him out of it."

"Did he die?"

"I always assumed so, but I couldn't reach any of his family and I never saw an obituary."

"Well, if he would try to talk you out of fighting this, then I'm glad he's not here," Leeanne said steadfastly.

II   PHILLIP HALMER

*J*oe was correct. If you spoke to 1,000 people that knew Phillip Halmer, you wouldn't be able to find one person that would say a bad word about him. He had blonde hair that was perhaps a bit longer than it needed to be, but it suited his carefree personality. With an infectious grin that ran from ear to ear, he was the guy other guys high-fived every time they saw him and the guy girls just had to hug. "Philly Bear" had that rare ability to make every person he came in contact with feel as though they were smart and funny—even if they weren't. People simply loved being around him.

And yet there was something that most people missed because he kept it so well hidden. He was a good student, but not a great one. He was a good athlete, but not a star. He was handsome, but not the guy every woman decided they needed to be with the moment he walked into a room. In fact, he was good at most things—just not the best at any of them—and that led to an inherent sadness within that only his closest friends noticed.

~

Phil gently waxed a ski in the back of his

otherwise empty shop with as much care as a newly minted mother might stroke her newborn. He was wearing Helly Hansen gear, the sign of a very good skier, not to be confused with someone who wanted to *look* like a very good skier by wearing a $3500 Kjus jacket. After college, he had moved out to Vail, where he became a ski instructor for the stars. Some of them wanted to learn how to ski black diamonds, others just wanted to have Phil ski up to them by the lodge as if they had just skied a black diamond.

A man entered the store. Older and distinguished. More professor than ski enthusiast. "You know a guy named, Joe Moretti?" he asked.

Phil looked up from what he was doing, surprised to hear the name from his past. "Sure. He and I went to high school together. Why?"

"He was talking about you."

"And you know this how?"

"It's my job to know."

"It's your job to be a nosey bastard?"

"That is *exactly* my job," the man answered with a smile.

"Does it pay well?"

"It pays in ways more valuable than monetary rewards."

"So why was Joe talking about me?" Phil asked.

"He's been having some serious health issues."

"Not cancer," Phil asked.

The man nodded slowly.

"Shit. Terminal?"

"Afraid so."

"That sucks. He was a good guy."

"Still is a good guy. He was talking about how you had a similar decision to make when you decided to take yourself off dialysis."

"Yeah," Phil said quietly.

"Maybe you should go talk to him?"

"I'm not sure he would want to hear from me."

"Why not?"

"I kind of cut him and all my friends off when I got sick. I didn't want to be judged."

"People have an amazing capacity to forgive where their friends are concerned."

"I dunno."

"It's up to you," the man said. "I just thought you'd want to know."

III   UNLIKELY FRIENDS

*J*oe Moretti and Phil Halmer became unlikely friends when Phil transferred into Joe's high school during Phil's junior year. Joe was only a freshman when they met for the first time during soccer pre-season in August. Phil was a good player. Joe was a great one. But if it bothered Phil that a freshman was starting over him, he never let it show. Phil was widely respected on the team, probably due in no small part to how he handled himself at all times.

Phil taught Joe how to drive a stick shift in his run-down Honda Civic. He taught him how to drink when he brought him to an upperclassmen party. And he drove him on his first date; a double date with Phil and two cheerleaders that had actually asked *them* out.

For his part, Joe had attended the K through 12 school since first grade, so there wasn't a student, teacher or staff member he didn't know, or who didn't owe him a favor of some kind, which enabled him to make Phil's transition to a new school smoother than it otherwise might have been.

What Joe valued most about his friendship

with Phil was that on a rainy day, when there was absolutely nothing exciting going on in the world, they could talk for hours about everything and nothing at all. Everyone had "social" friends that they enjoyed going out with, as well as friends they could confide in during times of stress. When you found that rare person that filled both voids, that was the definition of a best friend.

High school wasn't the same once Phil graduated and headed off to college, but no matter how much time had passed, whenever they got together, it was as if they had seen each other only the day before. They remained in touch when Phil moved out to Vail, and reunited when Joe moved to Los Angeles after college. Phil was the first person to visit him when he moved out West, making the 14 hour drive for a long weekend.

They headed to the racetrack as soon as he arrived, placing $4 bets on the ponies and celebrating as if they had won the Kentucky Derby when they finally hit an Exacta that paid $12.94. They drove back to Joe's apartment jamming to 80's tunes that only people of that era could fully appreciate, so engrossed in the music that Joe wasn't paying attention when he was forced into a left turn only lane instead of going straight towards the 405 freeway.

Forty-five minutes later when they eased into a parking spot beneath Joe's building in Sherman Oaks, they sensed something was wrong. The streets were empty at 6:30 in the evening and they could hear Joe's phone ringing off the hook from downstairs.

It was his mother asking if they were all right, and when he wondered why they wouldn't be, she had him turn on the television. Splashed all over the news was video of a truck driver named Reginald Denny, being pulled from his truck and beaten within an inch of his life for no reason other than being in the wrong place at the wrong time. That wrong place was two blocks away and on the same road from where they had been cut off and forced to turn.

The LA Riots as they would become known, had started after white officers on trial for police brutality of a black man had been acquitted. Billows of smoke from buildings that had been lit on fire out of anger could be seen and smelled from 20 miles away, and when the fires spread into Hollywood and headed toward the Valley, Phil decided it was time to hot foot it out of town.

"I'll see you in a few weeks," he said as they made plans for Joe to join him on the ski slopes of Vail.

"See you in a few weeks. Maybe sooner if this continues," Joe answered.

When they man-hugged goodbye, Joe had no idea it would be the last time he would ever see his friend. A few weeks later, Phil became sick. His kidneys were failing, and he had a host of other health issues that prevented him from getting on a donor list. The alternative was dialysis four times a week, which was a draining and time consuming process that limited his ability to work, and significantly lowered his quality of life.

Joe made plans to visit him anyway, but Phil told him to wait until he was feeling better. The problem was he never got better, and eventually, he stopped returning Joe's calls altogether. About a year later, he heard through a mutual friend that Phil had decided to take himself off dialysis. And then he heard nothing at all. It was as if his friend had vanished into thin air.

IV AN UNEXPECTED VISITOR

*T*he bowling alley was empty save for one lone bowler on lane 17. Joe always practiced on his lucky number lane, throwing ball after ball down the aisle, trying to replicate the same motion and footwork with each roll.

He held his hands over the blower on the ball return, rubbing his fingers back and forth, for what reason he had no idea. When his ball popped out of the chute, he removed it and cupped it purposefully in his hand. He leaned forward, looked down to make sure his feet were in their proper place, then began his approach. Joe's arm extended backwards and had just begun to swing forward when—

"I could have pictured you doing a lot of things. Lawyer. Politician. Businessman. Hedge Fund guy. Professor. But professional bowler? I wouldn't have guessed that if you gave me a football season worth of Saturdays to try."

Joe's head swung around at the sound of the eerily familiar voice and he released the ball sooner than he had planned. It clunked into and out of the gutter, popped onto the next lane over, and ended as a strike.

"Nice shot. You practice that?" the man said.

"What the—" Joe said, stunned.

"Now that I think about it," the man continued, "you never were much of a dresser. Those bowling shirts probably fit in perfectly with the rest of your wardrobe."

"Phil?"

"Yes, sir."

"But I thought you were..."

"Dead?"

"Yeah," Joe nodded.

"As Mark Twain once said, *reports of my death are greatly exaggerated.*"

"Last I heard, you were taking yourself off dialysis."

"I did. But then a distant relative came forward and gave me a kidney."

"I must have tried reaching you a thousand times."

"Yeah, I'm sorry about that. I was in kind of a dark place for a while."

"But you're ok now?"

"Good as gold."

"I can't believe it," Joe said, a broad grin sweeping across his face. He scooped Phil into the air and spun him around like a rag doll.

They were both laughing now.

"What do you say we get a drink?" Joe asked.

"At 10:30 in the morning?"

"It's Happy Hour somewhere." He put his arm around his friend as they approached the bar. "Mary. Line up a couple of your best lagers for my friend and me."

"That would be Bud Light," Mary responded. She was in her fifties, a bit unhappy with her station in life, but too comfortable to do anything to change it.

"Then Bud Light it is for my best friend!" Almost as an afterthought, he added, "Are you allowed to drink?"

"Within reason," Phil answered.

"I still can't believe you're here," Joe said as they settled into a couple of bar stools. "I was *just* talking to my wife about you the other day."

"About my dashing good looks and how glad you are she met you first or she would have ended up with me?"

"Definitely not."

"Ouch."

"Actually, I've been having some health problems and I was telling her about your decision."

"Serious ones?"

"Yeah."

"Not cancer?"

Joe nodded silently.

"Is it treatable?"

"It's treatable," Joe answered. "Not that it would make much difference."

"What kind of odds are they giving you?"

"Let's just say they named a Robert Downey Jr. movie after them."

"Iron Man?" Phil asked, confused.

"Less Than Zero."

"Jesus. I'm sorry, buddy. We saw that movie together," he said with a wry smile.

"I know. But hey, that's life, right?"

"How long have you got?"

"Six to ten months if I don't do chemo. Maybe a year or two if I do."

"Why wouldn't you do it?"

Joe took a generous swig of his beer. He had obviously been giving it a lot of thought. "Because I don't want to be a burden to Leeanne. I remember how difficult it was on my mother when my father's health went the last few years he was alive."

"Do you think your mother wouldn't have married him if she knew how it would end? I'm fairly certain the highs far outweighed the lows."

"I'm sure you're right, but I don't want to be remembered as some pissed off, withering old fool," Joe explained.

"Well, buddy, I'm not sure that would change no matter what you decide," Phil said, an impish grin stretching across his face.

"HA. HA."

"What if you don't get the chemo and they find a cure for cancer two months after you die?"

"They haven't found a cure for more than 5,000 years. I somehow doubt an extra two months would make much of a difference. Then again, with my luck, that's exactly what would happen."

"Are you kidding? With your luck, they'll be reading you your last rites, and a doctor will come flying into the room with cure serum."

Joe laughed out loud.

"What about your wife?"

"What about her?"

"Don't you want to spend as much time as possible with her?"

"If it was quality time, of course. You, of all people, should know about that. You decided to take yourself off dialysis because your quality of life had diminished too much."

He was correct on that, but Phil remained undaunted. "True. But it was a different situation. I had been on dialysis for a very long time and it had gotten to the point where I couldn't even hold down a job. It wasn't much of a life. But here's the thing. I got really lucky. But if I had come off dialysis one week before I did, I wouldn't be here right now."

Joe nodded. He wasn't convinced, but it did give him something to think about.

"Ok. Thinking a little outside the box for a moment, what if, and this is hypothetical obviously, but what if a year from now, someone was in need of help that only you could provide, and what if you weren't around to give it?"

"What kind of help? I'm pretty sure there are other people that could teach them how to pick up a 6-10 split."

"I don't know what kind. Maybe it would be right place at the right time. Maybe it would be someone you haven't even met yet. Maybe it would be your destiny."

"I think you're reaching a bit," Joe said as he motioned to Mary for a refill.

"Tell you what. After we finish this round, what do you say we head to the Mets game? I've never been to Citi Field. We can continue this conversation there, or not, if you don't want to."

~

The stadium was half empty as it usually was for a Thursday afternoon game, and they were able to pick up great seats pretty cheaply from a scalper as they stepped off the 7 line. They were in the Hyundai Club, the balcony level seats behind home plate, which included an all you can eat buffet, a private cash bar, a private bathroom, and a private entrance to their seats.

"Roasted chicken. Grilled salmon. Penne a la vodka. Bacon wrapped hot dogs. A fully stocked bar. Are you kidding me? Whatever happened to a hot dog, beer and peanuts in the upper deck?"

"Baseball has become less of a sport and more of an exclusive Roman Orgy-type event," Joe explained.

"Remember when we used to smuggle in a case of beer in a backpack? Then we'd buy one round from the concessions so we would have the proper cups and drink all day for $17.99 for us both."

"I'm afraid those days went away after 9-11. You can't smuggle a toothbrush in these days."

Joe was putting mustard on a hot pretzel when

a foul ball soared high into the air and landed a couple of rows back. It rattled around for a moment before settling beneath the seat directly behind them. No one was seated there, but a woman came charging down the row, only to be met with a solid hip check from Joe, who sent her flying into the next row. No part of her was happy as Joe picked the ball up and handed it to a delighted little boy in front of them.

"That's why I love these seats. Always good for a foul ball or two. I once got three in the same game. Ended up on ESPN."

"That woman was not pleased," Phil laughed. "You sent her flying."

"Well, here's the thing. I learned my lesson a few years ago. I was sitting down by the dugout one night and David Wright was jogging off the field after catching a pop up to 3rd. He pointed to the boy next to me and tossed him the ball. I leaned out of the way so the kid could catch it, and some drunk a-hole knocked five people out of the way including his girlfriend and snatched the ball. So I decided to never again back off a ball. If I can get it, I get it, and then I give it away."

"I guess there is some sort of twisted logic to that," Phil responded.

Leeanne picked them up from the train station when they returned to Connecticut after the game.

"I've heard a lot about you," she said, trying to be friendly but concerned as to what influence

Phil was having over her husband's decision.

"And me about you," Phil answered. "Joe has always been an overachiever where the ladies were concerned.   And my friend, you have really outdone yourself this time."

He had an easy way about him that enabled him to pay compliments to all sorts of people without it seeming as though he was sucking up or insincere.

"You are welcome to stay as long as you like," Leeanne said with a bright smile. "As long as you talk some sense into your friend."

"I've been trying to do that all day."

"How long can you stay?" Joe asked in an effort to shift the focus.

"I'm afraid I have to be in Boston tomorrow."

"What are you doing for work? Still teaching Hollywood types how to ski?"

"That, and I opened a sporting goods store. Have to meet with one of my suppliers tomorrow. But I'll definitely be back again soon, I promise."

"No more disappearing acts," Joe stated.

"No more," Phil promised.

V RUNNING WATER

*P*aul Ward and Charlie Dyjek met in the school jazz band in 10ᵗʰ grade. Paul played bass guitar while Charlie was a keyboard wizard. While they enjoyed playing some jazz and rhythm and blues, their true passion was to create their own band and a musical sound that fell somewhere between the college alternative sounds of REM and the grunge rock of Pearl Jam. They grabbed Charlie's little brother from the school marching band to play the drums, and Paul created smooth, yet driving melodies, but they sounded like three cats screeching on a hot tin roof when they tried to sing.

A lead singer was a must, but they had no luck until a boy from their class named Adam, appeared at the fall talent show singing Puccini's *Nessun Dorma* and blew them all away. They didn't even know who he was. He didn't exactly run in their circle of friends. Or any circle of friends for that matter. Adam was raised by a single mother, who allowed him to leave the house for school or school related functions only. As Paul tried to visualize how to transform this boy's tenor voice into an alt rock singing sensation, Mother Nature stepped in and did it for him in the form of puberty. The boy's now lower, gravely voice fit perfectly with their musical stylings.

They practiced in Paul's garage after school, the greatest challenge being convincing Adam's mother that what they were doing was for a school project. The following year, they won the talent show, and were asked to play at the school's Spring Fling. Soon after, they were playing other other high school proms, and three years later, they were a major fixture on the college band circuit, playing gigs at nearby schools on the weekends, while college radio stations gave them tons of airtime.

Running Water, as they named themselves, received their big break when the lead singer for the opening act for Depeche Mode overdosed in his hotel room the day they were scheduled to play the Oakdale Theatre in Wallingford, Connecticut. Scrambling to find a replacement act on short notice, someone who went to high school with them, handed the event organizer a recording of the band. They had less than an hour to get to the arena and no time even for a sound check, but it didn't matter. *Running Water* rocked it anyway.

They signed with Capitol Records a week later, and the rest, as they say, was history. Their first studio album hit #1 on the charts, and they toured sold out popular venues from Red Rocks to the Saratoga Performing Arts Center and

Madison Square Garden. They made decent money for the day, although not the millions that the top bands of the future would make. But it didn't stop them from spending money as if they did. Huge after show parties, penthouse hotel rooms, ridiculous cars even though they rarely drove themselves anywhere.

Their manager did his best to keep them grounded, but it was an uphill climb. Even the quietly reserved Adam, who hadn't kissed a girl until he was past his 21st birthday, was soon mixing shots of whiskey with lines of coke off strippers chests. Rave reviews of his unique singing voice and three platinum albums did little to keep his ego in check.

After five years of non-stop touring and a week long hospital stay following a near death overdose, Adam Harper left the band. There were reports that he really had died from the overdose. Another said he was living on the streets of New York City. Other reports had him sighted in various odd places throughout the globe. One even claimed he had moved to the deep south and become a pastor at a remote episcopal church. Two things were certain. The first was that he was never heard from publicly again. The second was that *Running Water* would never be as successful again.

VI   AN EVEN MORE UNEXPECTED VISITOR

*B*ianca Foster's idea of a night out was to play a rousing game of Political Password with a couple of her girlfriends. In fairness to her, as a 3rd year resident at Yale-New Haven Hospital, free time was a luxury she didn't have much of. So it was that much more surprising when she asked a co-worker to switch shifts with her so she could attend the *Depeche Mode/Running Water* reunion concert at The Meadows.

The original concert 14 years earlier, was the first one she ever attended, back when the headliner was at the peak of its popularity and *Running Water* was a last minute fill in band to open the show.   But as was always the case whenever she went anywhere, Bianca made her parents drive her and a couple of friends to the show an hour early and she fell in love with the opening act.

Every person had a band that "spoke to them" and for Bianca, that band was *Running Water*. She cried when their lead singer left and celebrated more than when she was accepted to Harvard when they reunited, albeit with a different front man--whose vocal limitations made it impossible for him to sing her favorite song. Whenever she was having a bad day, she need only drown her sorrows with a merlot and the sounds of their first album and all was good in the world once again. It was safe to say that she was looking forward to the reunion concert more than just about anything else she could remember.

~

Bianca was two hours into her morning shift on the day of the show, when news was called in that a bus had overturned on 95 and dozens of injured people were headed to the hospital. Her first thought was hoping none of the injuries were serious enough to delay her departure for the concert. She was waiting at the Emergency Room entrance with a half dozen other doctors and nurses when the cavalcade of ambulances pulled up.

Three years of medical school and three years of residency had prepared her for a lot of things, but the sight of the lead singer of her favorite band being wheeled in on a stretcher wasn't one of them. She even thought her eyes were deceiving her until the other three members walked in on their own power after him. Pausing only briefly to compose herself as if she were set to operate on a family member or close friend, she prepped quickly and headed in for surgery.

Nearly five hours later, she entered the seldomly used private waiting room where the other members of *Running Water* were waiting.

"How are you all?" Bianca asked.

"No worries here," Paul said. "Just a couple of cuts and bruises, but your staff patched us right up. How's Mike?"

"He's pretty banged up. He suffered a punctured lung, a lacerated kidney and a couple of broken bones, but he's going to be ok," she said.

"Thank god," Paul responded. "And thank you, Doctor."

"You're more than welcome. Just doing my job," she answered, knowing full well this surgery was far more than that for her.

Andrew remained seated with his face buried in his hands.

"Did you hear her?" Paul asked. "He's going to be fine."

"I did," Andrew said, looking up glumly. "And I'm really grateful for that."

"Then why the pout?"

Andrew sat in silence for a moment or two as he tried to decide whether to say anything or keep it to himself. "This is going to sound really bad," he said at last. "I'm really happy Mike's going to be ok. But I was really counting on this tour to get me out of debt. I know Mike was too. His house is about to be foreclosed on."

"How can that be?" Charlie asked.

"When we were making good money, I spent it like we were always going to be making it. And Mike came in after our best days were already behind us. This tour was going to be our chance at a comfortable life."

"Maybe we can find someone to fill in with us?" Paul offered. "And raise some money for Mike in the process."

"Who are we going to get at the last minute that would be familiar enough with our material to sing live?"

The words were still floating in the air when the double doors of the room were thrown open and a man entered. The hallway lighting in the background made it difficult to make out who it was at first, but it became clearer as the doors closed behind him. His hair was shorter and he had a few more wrinkles around his eyes and forehead, but his smile was unmistakable. The collective jaws on the three original members of the band hit the floor and none of them could utter a word upon seeing Adam Harper standing before them. Bianca did one better when she fainted at the very sight of him.

VII   THE SHOW MUST GO ON

"*W*ho's the girl?" Adam asked, as he looked at an unconscious Bianca lying across Paul's lap.

"She is Mike's doctor," Paul answered.

"Not a very inspiring sight."

"Where the hell did you come from?" Andrew asked accusingly.

"What are you doing here?" Charlie wondered.

"How did you find us?" Paul questioned.

"Where I came from is a bit complicated," Adam explained. "What I'm doing here is seeing if you guys were all right. As for how I found you. That was easy. It's been all over the news."

"What are you doing in Connecticut?" Paul followed.

"I'm back home looking after my mother."

"And you thought you'd just show up and everything would be forgiven?"

"I never for one minute, thought that I could make things right by just showing up. But everyone has to start somewhere."

"You left us high and dry."

"I'm sorry about that, I really am. But I was

out of control back then and if I hadn't left when I did, I'd probably be dead now," Adam reasoned.

"The press thinks you already are."

"They also think Elvis and Tupac are alive."

"I went to your funeral," Andrew said.

"So did I," Charlie said.

"I didn't. You ungrateful bastard," Paul said. "So what are you *really* doing here?"

"I already told you," Adam answered. "But I couldn't help but overhear your conversation when I was coming in. Maybe I could help?"

"You want to sing with us again?!" Paul responded scornfully.

"I do know all the songs."

"And he could sing my favorite song," Bianca interjected. She had been awake for a few moments, but kept quiet because she was comfortable with her head resting on Paul's lap.

"You know who we are?" Paul asked.

"Of course I do. I'm your biggest fan."

"What's your favorite song?" Charlie asked.

"What I'd Be Without You."

"Yeah, Mike's great, but he can't quite hit the notes required for that song," Paul explained.

"I could help just until Mike is back. I could help you guys make some money," Adam said.

You could almost see each of them weighing the pros and cons in their minds. Waiting for one of them to take the lead.

"The first show is supposed to be in an hour and a half in Hartford. And we don't even have a way of getting there," Paul said.

"I could drive you," Bianca offered. "I was planning to go to the show anyway."

"You could fit us all?"

"Sure. I have an SUV. But I don't think I'd be able to fit any equipment."

"The equipment is already there. It went in a separate truck."

"Well?" Adam wondered.

Paul, Charlie and Andrew shared a couple of looks. Andrew nodded. Charlie shrugged. Paul reluctantly agreed.

"Ok, I guess," he said at last. It wasn't a ringing endorsement, but it was a start.

They arrived at the venue 45 minutes before the show, which left them with just enough time to clean up and grab something to eat.

"We should probably stick to the old stuff," Paul said as he handed a set list to Adam.

"I know some of the new stuff too," Adam responded.

Paul nodded. He was impressed, even if he didn't want to show it.

The guys got Bianca and her friends in the first row, directly in front of the stage.

"I love these guys," a man of about Bianca's age said. It was half to no one in particular, and half directed at her.

He was cute. Tall. Tightly cropped, neat hair. Clean shaven. Fantastic smile.

"Well it wouldn't make much sense coming if you didn't," she answered, her guard up as always.

The man wasn't fazed. "Fair point," he smiled. "I'm Jack Doyle."

He offered his hand to her and she noticed it had remnants of what appeared to be grease on it.

"I promise you I washed my hands," he said. "Some of it is a little built in."

"So what do you do, Jack Doyle?"

"I'm a doctor," he replied.

"Oh really?" she said doubtfully. "Whereabouts?"

"Down in Milford."

"Milford Hospital? I'm actually a doctor at Yale-New Haven."

"Not Milford Hospital."

She continued her tough line of questioning. "Where then?"

"You've probably never heard of it."

"Well, what's your specialty?"

"I'm a doctor of automobiles," he answered with a smile. "I've never lost a patient yet."

Bianca felt her normally substantial wall crumbling down around her. Jack had a disarming quality about him that made it impossible to not like him.

The lights went dim, and a spotlight kicked on to the shrieks of the crowd, which was completely full.

"Good evening, ladies and gentlemen!" Paul began enthusiastically. "So some of you may have heard that we had a little trouble on our way to the show today. Don't worry, Mike is ok, thanks to a new friend of ours. And he wanted this show to go on, so we are going to do exactly that, with the help of an old friend--Mr. Adam Harper!"

The crowd went wild. Off the rails wild. Even more so when the first few chords of *What I'd Be Without You* were heard.

"This one is for Bianca," Adam crooned.

"Oh. My. God." she gushed. She reached over and grabbed Jack. "I have to dance to this!"

He didn't put up any resistance as she pulled him close and rested her head on his shoulder. Bianca was in heaven. Jack Doyle was in love.

VIII   DESTINARE

*S*ix months after their first dance, Bianca and Jack were married. One year after that, they had a baby girl they named Diana, after his mother. Precocious. Blue-eyed. Full of curls.

Although work remained one of her priorities, it now wasn't her only one and she made certain to set aside time for her family. On one such day, they were headed by train to New York City to see the Christmas Tree Lighting ceremony at Rockefeller Plaza.

Also on the Milford platform that morning was Joe Moretti. He had decided to follow his friend's advice and began chemotherapy shortly after they spoke. Four years later, he had far exceeded the doctor's life expectancies for him. For the most part, he had felt decently, although a bit tired and worn out in the days that immediately followed treatment. He and his wife traveled to Hawaii for the first time, and took a Mediterranean cruise to Venice, Rome and the Greek Islands of Santorini, Mykonos and Corfu. But his greatest accomplishment was that he and Leanne also had a child--a three year old boy named Nick.

The last few weeks had been a bit rough for Joe and he sensed the curtain on his final act was being prepared to be dropped, but he was determined to have his wife and son's final memories of him to be good ones. They too, were headed into New York City to see the lights but from atop the Empire State Building, a place he hadn't been since he was a small child. For his part, Phil kept his promise to return, coming back every month for a long weekend visit; although reaching him between visits was a near impossibility. He was with them on this day as well.

"The 3:07 southbound train to New York is on schedule and will arrive at the station in two minutes," the pre-recorded announcement droned.

Joe pulled the lapels of his peacoat tight and re-wrapped his scarf around his neck. The chemo killed cancer cells, but also his immune system, and he felt the bitter cold through every inch of his body.

"Are you ok?" Leanne asked.

"Yup. I'm good," he answered unconvincingly.

She knew he was lying.

Joe studied the others on the platform, hoping that by concentrating, it would distract him from the cold. He saw an older man, had to be in his late 80's with what looked to be his son and grandchildren. What a great but somewhat sad run he must have had, outliving his wife and all his friends. There were a couple of high schools kids there as well, most likely on a date fairly early in their relationship with their whole lives left in front of them. And then he saw precocious Diana Doyle walking the balance beam perilously close to the platform edge as her parents battled with the ticket selling machine ten feet away. No one else seemed to notice when she started to lose her balance and fell off the platform onto the tracks.

The train was coming in at that time, horn blaring which served to drown out Diana's screams for help. But Joe saw her fall. Mustering up every last ounce of energy he had in his 48 year old body, he jumped onto the tracks and began scurrying towards Diana. He reached her with the train about 300 yards away and the conductor screaming on the brakes with all his might. Joe scooped Diana up and would have carried her onto the other tracks, but wasn't sure which ones were "live". He made a split second decision to hoist her onto the platform while her parents ran over, having just figured out what was going on. He then tried to pull himself up as well, but there wasn't much to grab on to. Until an arm appeared. Phil's arm. Joe grasped his best friend's forearm with his hand and Phil helped hoist him onto the platform as the train eased past and eventually came to a halt.

"You ok, buddy?!" Phil asked.

"I can never thank you enough," Bianca gushed through tears as she bear hugged Diana.

Joe was exhausted and could only manage an arm wave and a thumbs up as he struggled to catch his breath.

"Do you think it would be ok if we went home instead?" he asked Leanne and Phil.

"Of course," she said with tears welled up in her eyes. She couldn't have been prouder of him.

Three hours later, Joe Moretti was gone. He passed in his sleep with a peaceful smile on his face.

IX TEDDY KERRIGAN

*T*he ring of Teddy Kerrigan's cell phone sounded much louder and more menacing when waking him from a sound sleep. It also sent a shiver down his spine because he knew that no good news was ever delivered at 6:30am.

Teddy reached down to the floor and unhooked the phone from the charger with one hand, before fumbling around for the little red button that answered it.

"Mom?? Is everything ok with you and dad?" he asked in a tone that sounded far more awake than he actually was.

"Your father and I are fine," she answered.

Teddy breathed a sigh of relief, while waiting for the inevitable word that would soon follow.

"But...Jim Holt died."

"When?"

"Two days ago apparently."

It was a straight shot to the gut.

"I didn't know he had been sick."

"He hadn't been. He had a stroke in his sleep."

"How old was he?"

"Sixty-five," his mother responded.

"That's awful," Teddy mumbled. "I wouldn't be where I am today without him."

"I know. That's why I called as soon as I found out in case you wanted to send flowers or write something for the funeral."

"When is the funeral?" Teddy asked.

"Tomorrow morning."

He mulled it over quickly in his mind. Some things were just too important to miss. "Forget flowers. Get my room ready. I'm coming home."

* * *

It was impossible to get anywhere easily from South Bend, Indiana. Teddy had to take a puddle jumper to Chicago. A tram to the other side of O'Hare. Another flight to New York. A bus to the rental car facility. And finally, a car for what should have been an hour drive to Connecticut, but took more than two because it was rush hour.

The town he grew up in, Fairfield, Connecticut, had changed quite a bit over the years—both for the better, and for the worse. What was at one time a middle class town in many respects, was now part of the Connecticut Gold Coast, with swanky "bistros" and wine bars, replacing pubs and mom and pop restaurants.

His parents still lived in town, although not in the house he grew up in. They certainly didn't go far, moving a full five streets over so they could have a house with a master bedroom on the ground floor as they grew older. He had visited them at the new house a couple of dozen times since they moved, but every single time he did, he had to drive by the old house first.

It was a beige, vinyl sided home with powder blue shutters and tall rectangular columns in the front. Like the street it was on, the house was comfortable, but not too big. It was the perfect house on the perfect street in the perfect town to raise a family. There were nearly a dozen kids Teddy's age growing up, and as he parked in the cul de sac at the top of the road and looked at the house, he was able to visualize the memories of home run derby, baseball, basketball and football in the back yards that blended into one big, long yard that ran the complete length of the street.

He smiled a reminiscent smile as he shifted the car into drive and made the five block journey to where his parents now lived. In many respects, the new house was nicer. It was larger, and newer with a swimming pool and all the modern amenities the house he grew up in lacked. But without the NFL football wallpaper and posters of Walt Frazier and Walter Payton in his bedroom, it was more hotel than home.

His parents were in the doorway as he pulled up, and probably had been for quite some time. Teddy waved to them and they smiled proudly, the way they had every time they had seen him since the day he was born. As he hugged them both together, it dawned on him that home wasn't about a house.   Home was simply wherever the people you loved were.

X   A TOUGH LESSON LEARNED

Teddy Kerrigan had been a three sport athlete in high school who had garnered interest from a host of Division I colleges for each sport he played until they realized he wasn't much of a student. His grades were really his choice. He attended every class because his parents would not have allowed it any other way, and he respected them too much to openly disobey them. But attending classes and actually paying attention in them were completely different animals.

Teachers passed him along because he was surprisingly bright, albeit extremely lazy, and he had an easy way about him that made it difficult to dislike him. Difficult, but not impossible.

"Mr. Kerrigan.   Trigonometry is NOT a spectator sport," Mr. Fujitsu announced one afternoon as he eased his way down the aisles of chairs checking out the notes of his students, only to find Teddy had none.

"That's good, Mr. F, because it wouldn't make a very entertaining one," Teddy answered.

The class roared and Mr. Fujitsu had fought enough battles with students in his 25+ years to know when he was outnumbered. He thought about saying something once the bell rang and students began pouring in and out of the classroom, but he decided it wasn't the right time.

Teddy stepped into the hallway surrounded, as he always was, by an entourage of friends and hangers on. He was the equivalent of a high school rock star. Everyone wanted to be around him. Most people wanted to *be* him.

"Mr. Kerrigan, I need to speak with you for a minute," said a tall, athletic looking man with salt and pepper hair wearing a suit that was probably worth more than the rest of the outfits of every teacher in the school combined.

"Nice threads, Mr. Holt," Teddy responded as he ran his hand down the fine fabric of the man's shoulder.

"Before you can play the part, you have to dress the part," the man answered. "Now about those grades of yours..."

"I'm doing ok."

"If your definition of ok is scraping through by the slimmest of margins."

"I'm eligible."

"Eligible isn't going to cut it in life. Not when you have the potential to be so much more than that," the man stated. "Listen, Mr. Kerrigan, I realize that being the cool guy in class might make you popular, and probably even gets you a few dates--"

"No one 'dates' anymore. We 'talk'."

"What does that even mean? I only ever see you guys playing games on that stupid computer.

But that's neither here nor there," he continued. "You have a great opportunity to make something of yourself. One that you don't seem to appreciate. I'd understand it more if you didn't have the capability to do well."

"I'm an ideas guy, Mr. Holt. I leave the execution of them to other people. I function best in a supervisory capacity."

"No one will be interested in ideas from a guy without a college degree."

"I'll get my degree."

"But where from?"

"I have a dozen DI scholarship offers," Teddy responded.

"And how many more passed on you because of your grades?"

"A few, I guess."

"A few?"

"Maybe a few more than a few."

"That's just not acceptable. More offers means better offers. Better offers means better opportunities either because you would be coming from a better school or have less debt when you come out. And to be completely honest, I'm concerned that you won't actually get your degree. Your laissez faire attitude will result in you flunking out. In college, it isn't good enough to show up. You need to take notes and actually do the work."

"I'll get by."

"And then what?"

"What do you mean and then what? What

else is there?"

"I don't mean to crap in your cornflakes, Mr. Kerrigan, but the NFL isn't in your future. So what you do in the classroom will determine what you do for the rest of your life."

"I'm not too worried about it."

"Of course you're not. People your age rarely are. But I tell you what. I'm going to do you an enormous favor. I'm going to let Coach Shea know that you are suspended from the team indefinitely until you start making a better effort in the classroom. If necessary, I'll let Coach Sharp know as well when basketball rolls around."

Teddy became indignant. "But I'm eligible!"

"By the state's standards, maybe. But not in this school. And not on my watch."

"You can't do that!"

"I can do whatever I want. I'm the principal," Mr. Holt said as he walked away.

If Teddy's parents were different, things might have gone differently, but they weren't like most people. They supported a principal that had ignored the easy publicity that came hand in hand with a winning football team and helped teach their son a valuable lesson in the process. They knew that enabling Teddy now would cripple him for the rest of his life. They were grateful for Mr. Holt, and they knew someday their son would be too. Just not then.

Teddy didn't speak to Mr. Holt once in the four months that followed, even after he was reinstated for the last five games of the football season and helped lead them to a conference championship. But he, along with his coach, his teammates, and many students and parents blamed Holt for costing the team a spot in the State Playoffs, after they lost a couple of early season games while Teddy sat out.

On the college front, Teddy's dream school was the same as every Irish Catholic football player in the country, and when Notre Dame's Lou Holtz rang the front doorbell of the Kerrigan household one evening, Teddy's life would change forever.

"I'm going to be honest with you, son," Coach Holtz said. "Last year, you weren't even on our radar. Oh, you were talented enough on the field. And your SAT scores were high enough. But your grades were lousy, and that told me you were lazy. And we just don't recruit lazy student-athletes at Notre Dame. But someone tipped me off to your situation here, so I started nosing around. Now I'm sure you're plenty pissed off that they held you out, but instead of being pissed, you should be grateful. Your principal and your parents taught you the value of hard work, and not wasting potential. And there is nothing, believe me, nothing, more wasteful than wasted potential. What they did for you, you will never ever be able to fully repay them for, but you can at least start with a simple *thank you*. It is because of them, and because of what I'm hoping you learned, that I'm offering you the opportunity to play football at the University of Notre Dame next fall."

Teddy sat in stunned silence before asking his mother to hand him the phone.

"Who do you have to call right now??" his mother asked.

"I need to call Mr. Holt," he answered.

His mother handed him the phone with a smile.

XI IN MEMORIAM

The line was three deep and had already wrapped around the church when Teddy pulled up, the way it did anytime someone young or someone who worked with young people had died. The police directed him to a side street where 40 or so cars were parked on both sides of the road.

As he approached, he searched the crowd for a familiar face--a classmate, a former teacher, a coach--but didn't see any. It had been 22 years since he had graduated and a lot had changed since then. His classmates and teammates were now scattered all over the country living their own lives, and many no longer had ties to the area. They might not have even known of Mr. Holt's passing.

And then, a tap on his shoulder. "Teddy?"

He turned at the sound of the soothing voice and found himself staring into eyes as blue as he remembered them. Eyes so blue they had their own nickname. The Betsy Blues, the name for the wholesome girl next door looking daughter of the former principal. Betsy was two years younger than Teddy, which was nothing now, but would have left him the subject of ridicule back in high school.

"Betsy," he exclaimed sadly. "I can't tell you how sorry I was to hear about your dad. He was a great man."

She hugged him tightly. "He would be so happy to know you were here," she said.

"Well, as awkward as this will sound given that it is a funeral, I wouldn't have missed it."

"Would you do me a favor and say a few words during the service? I was going to call you, but wasn't sure if you were going to make it and didn't want to put any undo pressure on you to come since I know how busy you are. But now that you're here..." her voice trailed off.

How could he say no? "Of course," Teddy answered. "I'd be honored."

"Excellent," she said as she grabbed his hand and lead him through the crowd into the church where her family was waiting.

He felt awkward for a split second being led away by a 16 year old cheerleader, but then he realized she hadn't been 16 for more than 20 years. Where had the days gone?

"Mom. Look who made it??"

"Oh my god. Teddy Kerrigan! Thank you so much for coming," Jim Holt's wife exclaimed with a welcoming hug.

"I'm really sorry," was all Teddy could muster.

"Thank you. We're all going to miss him terribly. Teddy. Let me introduce you to my brother, Joe. Teddy graduated from Martin and is now the athletic director at the University of--"

"--Notre Dame," Joe interrupted. "I know exactly who he is. I saw you interviewed at half time of the USC game a few weeks ago."

"Oh lord," Teddy said. "They only want to talk to the AD when something goes wrong."

"Yeah, they were asking you about the guys that were thrown off the team for getting in a bar fight."

"I hope I didn't come across as too much of a jerk."

"You were great. I wish more schools held their athletes to higher standards."

"So Teddy has agreed to say a few words," Betsy interjected, and suddenly, thoughts of Notre Dame had become nothing but a distant memory for him.

"That's really nice of you. It will be great to get the perspective of one of his former students," Mrs. Holt answered.

Betsy insisted he enter the church with the family, but he felt awkward about it. All he could think about was how there was a body inside the cherry oak box on wheels in front of them. A body that had been full of life as recently as a few days ago. Teddy had never had many brushes with death in his 40 years, save for losing one of his grandparents. He barely remembered his mother's father, who passed when Teddy was just five and he never knew his other grandparents, all of whom had died before Teddy had even been a glint in his mother's eye.

In fact, he had attended fewer than a dozen funerals in his lifetime, all in support of friends, and none had hit home like this one. It was his first brush with mortality. Until the organist started the procession, he had never really given death much of a thought. His parents, teachers, coaches, and friends had always just been there and he felt as though they always would be. But seeing Betsy and her family up close like that with tears in their collective eyes made him realize just how fleeting life could be.

Teddy made his way to the podium in the packed church. Even with no one speaking, it was noisy with shuffling programs, creaking pews, and the occasional cough.

"Years ago," Teddy began, "far more than I'd like to admit, I once asked Jim Holt exactly what the responsibility of a principal was. Teachers teach," I said. "Coaches coach. The Vice Principals deal with grades and discipline. What exactly is it that you do?"

Mr. Holt laughed his hearty laugh and responded, "My job is to be like Magellan, guiding the staff through uncharted waters, without actually steering the boat myself."

"And guide us he did. He pushed for the inclusion of girls into what had previously been an all boys school. He oversaw fundraising for projects that included a new turf stadium for football, soccer and lacrosse. He used athletics to increase enrollment and raise money for the arts and a state of the art theatre. And he raised the academic standards of the school with a top notch faculty. Mr. Holt was just as easily spotted at a math league contest or debate club meeting, as he was at the Homecoming football game. He was a husband, a father, a mentor, and a friend to everyone in this room. Along with my parents, he was the single biggest influence in my life. I owe much of the success I have had to his utter refusal to accept any less than the maximum potential he saw in a person. I only wish I had let him know that sooner and more often. But I guess we often take for granted that there will always be another time for that--until suddenly there isn't. The world will definitely be a worse place with Jim Holt no longer in it, but we are all better people for having the opportunity to know him at all. He will be missed."

When he was finished, he awkwardly attempted to walk back to his seat as quickly and quietly as possible, but found the more he tried to be quiet, the louder it seemed. He sat down next to Betsy in the front of the church and any question he had as to whether his tribute was fitting dissipated when she reached over and grasped his hand.

Thirty to forty cars made the drive to the cemetery on the bright, sunny morning and Teddy couldn't help but wonder at the contradiction of it all. Some people were likely having one of their best days, enjoying the beautiful late autumn day, while this group of 50 or so people were having one of their worst.

As the monotone priest droned on in the background, Teddy studied the faces of those in attendance. Some were openly sobbing. Others were fighting back tears. Most wore a solemn expression that couldn't very easily be described, but you knew the look when you saw it.

Sadness in general bothered Teddy. Not so much his own sadness. That he could deal with. But seeing others upset made him uncomfortable to the point where he had to look at the ground, as if he could find solace in those blades of grass.

One by one, people made their way to the casket to place a flower on top of it and say a prayer. He found it strangely odd that people would kneel before a closed wooden box, and couldn't help but wonder how many of those same people would have a heart attack on the spot, if the casket lid was thrown open and the person inside suddenly sat up straight. Teddy was certainly grateful it didn't happen while he was kneeling in front of it.

"You have to come back to the house for the luncheon reception," Besty whispered.

Teddy nodded that he would, and when she asked if he remembered where their house was, he nodded again, unsure of the etiquette of speaking at the end of a funeral.

He made his way to his rental car, when he heard the sound of a deep and familiar voice behind him.

"Trigonometry is not a spectator sport, Mr.

Kerrigan," Mr. Fujitsu bellowed.

Teddy turned with a smile. "That's good, because it wouldn't make a very entertaining one," he answered with a wink. "It's good to see you, Mr. F. You're retired now, aren't you?"

"Have been for nearly five years now."

"Do you miss it?"

"I'll always miss it. It's one of the few occupations where you really feel as though you can make a difference."

"And that you did. I know we didn't always show our appreciation, but you were a great teacher. You weren't afraid to tell us what we *needed* to hear, instead of what we *wanted* to hear. We also knew whenever we got a compliment from you, it was genuine. And I mean that in a good way."

"I appreciate that. I really do. I always wondered as a teacher if I was making an impact."

"You were."

"Well, thank you," he said, before adding after a slight pause, "So what about you?"

"What about me?"

"Do you miss your old hometown?"

"Of course. It was a great place to grow up."

"Then why don't you come back?"

"Well, I have a pretty good job," Teddy answered.

"Cmon, Kerrigan. It's not like you're the AD at the University of Michigan," Fujitsu winked in a nod to his own alma mater.

"Mr. F, I thought with age was supposed to

come wisdom? Shouldn't you be really, really, really wise by now?"

"Ever the smart ass, eh, Kerrigan?"

"Everyone's got to be good at something," he answered with a smile.

"There's a pretty good job open here right now."

Teddy looked confused. "You mean, Mr. Holt's?"

"Exactly."

"I'm an athletic director, not a high school principal."

"You can't tell me that running one of the largest and most profitable college athletic programs in the country wouldn't qualify you to run a catholic high school."

"I'm sure there will be plenty of qualified people that apply."

"Qualified people can't afford to work at Bishop Martin. They don't have the financial stability."

"What makes you think I do?"

"Give me a break, Kerrigan. You've made enough money to last five lifetimes."

"I don't know about that," Teddy shrugged. Three maybe, he thought to himself.

"So how about it?"

"I don't know. I'm pretty content."

"Content? Listen, I'm sure you're good at your job, and I don't mean to offend you, but that school and that athletic department would go on just fine without you. Here, you would have a chance to make a real difference."

"I'll think about it."

"If you have to think about it, you're not thinking clearly," Fujitsu responded. "Why'd you come here today?"

"To pay my respects to a good man who was a big influence in my life."

"What better way to pay tribute than to continue what he started?"

"Jesus. Hard sell much?" Teddy laughed as the wheels began turning in his head.

XII   MR. F'S BROTHER

"I hate these things," Teddy told Betsy matter-of-factly while they sat in her childhood swing set at her parent's home.

She burst into laughter.   "It's a funeral! Nobody likes them."

"I know but, in addition to missing the person who died, there's all this extra pressure. Should you go or not? What if you haven't been in touch with them for a long time? Are people going to wonder why you're there? What if they were just a casual acquaintance, but you always respected them a lot? What if you only know one of the family members? You want to support them, but feel ridiculous going through the receiving line and speaking to twenty other relatives you don't know. And then once you figure all that out, what do you say? Sorry for your loss? He or she was a great person? Why can't people just go with the honest approach? I never really liked him or her much, but I like him or her a lot more today."

"If you didn't like the person, why would you even go?" Betsy laughed.

"Because I think people appreciate the truth. Listen,   they know if their mom, dad, sister, brother, or friend was a jerk."

"I'm not so sure about that. People are sensitive where relatives are concerned."

"Ok, but what if you didn't like the person who died, but really like one of their relatives? Should you go and support them?"

"Is that why you came to today?" she asked.

"Of course not. I liked your dad way more than I like you," he answered with a wink.

"Part of your truthful approach?"

"Nah. I'm just teasin. I can't imagine anyone not liking the Betsy Blues."

"Why, thank you," she said as her face turned a slight crimson before she added, "So how come you never asked me out when we were younger if that was the case?"

"Are you kidding? Your dad would have killed me."

"My dad loved you."

"He loved me as long as I was a safe distance from his daughter."

"Well, you did work your way through half the cheerleading squad..."

"Incorrect. Only four of them."

"Only four? It seemed like a lot more from where I was standing. And what about these days? Still a playboy?"

"Not at all. My job is not very conducive to having a successful relationship. Plus, I moved around a lot after college and no one wanted to deal with that. And now, I call South Bend, Indiana home, and that is not exactly a destination hot spot. What about you?" He motioned to her bare wedding finger. "Not married?"

"I was. Once. But we were young. Just out of college. We grew apart."

"No kids?"

"No, thank god. I mean, I love kids, but it would have made the break up a lot more complicated."

"Anyone now?"

"I've been dating someone, but it isn't that serious. He teaches at Martin with me."

"Does he think it's serious?"

"What are you, the Spanish Inquisition?" she laughed.

Betsy swung a little higher on the swing in an effort to mask the awkward silence. Teddy hated silence.

"Ok fine," he began. "Change of subject. Have you given any thought to following in your father's footsteps?"

"As the Principal?" she asked.

"Yes."

She shook her head. "I'm a teacher. Teachers teach. I already hate how much being a department chair takes me out of the classroom."

Teddy fidgeted slightly. "I ran into Mr. Fujitzu at the cemetery. He suggested that maybe I throw in for the position."

"Somehow I doubt that," she answered flatly.

"You doubt he suggested that?"

"I doubt you ran into him."

"You doubt I ran into him?" he asked.

"Well, yeah, considering he died three years ago."

"Sure seemed pretty alive to me when I was talking to him about an hour ago."

She reached over and felt his forehead. "You don't feel warm."

"I'm not warm. And I wasn't hallucinating."

"Maybe you confused him with Mr. Perez."

"I can tell the difference between a smaller Japanese man, and a large Spanish guy," Teddy said, shaking his head.

"You know what? I bet it was Mr. F's brother!" she exclaimed.

"I didn't know he had a brother."

"Twin brother. Teaches at Fairfield High."

"I don't think so. The first thing he said was 'Trigonometry is not a--'"

"--spectator sport. Yes, I remember. They probably shared a lot of the same sayings."

"How would he even know who I was?"

"Not to feed your already inflated ego, but everyone knows who you are. You were a three-sport athlete. One of the best in school history. And you're the AD at Notre Dame now."

"I don't know," he said doubtingly. "I'm not buying it."

"I was at Mr. F's funeral," she countered.

It was hard to refute that. He replayed the conversation in his mind. He supposed it could have been his brother. He never made a direct reference either way. But he also didn't indicate he wasn't Mr. F.

"So what do you think?" she asked.

"About?"

"About taking over as Principal, duh."

"I could be interested."

"You'd be making about one tenth of the salary."

"I've never made work decisions based on money."

"Easier to do when you already have plenty of it," she smiled.

"Well, there is that," he responded, returning her smile.

"And there would be the added bonus of getting to see me every day!" she exclaimed.

"If you think you'd get any favored treatment because we are friends, you've got another thing coming."

"Oh please. You could never refuse the Betsy Blues."

"I most certainly could," he answered in what was probably the biggest lie of his life.

XIII JOEY BUTTONS

Teddy Kerrigan's decision to leave Notre Dame was the headline story on ESPN for about half a day, before being relegated to the back pages of newspapers everywhere outside of the Midwest.

"I love both of my alma maters," he explained, "but right now, I think my high school needs me more."

He soon became a footnote in Notre Dame's storied lore when a former Heisman Trophy winning quarterback decided to accept his old job. And with that, he packed up ten years of memories and headed back home to Connecticut.

He stayed with his parents until his house in Indiana sold, to the new AD ironically, and then bought a stately brick, Georgian-style estate overlooking a golf course in the Greenfield Hill section of Fairfield. It was the exclusive area of a wealthy town that was home to GE, hedge fund managers, and other Wall Street types. But when GE planned a move out of state and the housing bubble burst, homes in this area began to sell well below market value and in some instances, were foreclosed upon as families found themselves overextended.   As a result, Teddy was able to practically "steal" the house.   It was about five minutes from Bishop Martin and fifteen from his parents, boasting a gunite pool, with a bluestone patio and elevated deck with a hot tub.   The interior was an ode to times past with multiple fireplaces, a long, arching staircase in the front entry, and beautiful trim and crown molding in each room.   The library boasted floor to ceiling bookshelves, oriental throw rugs underneath a pair of leather arm chairs and a grand piano, even though Teddy couldn't play a note.   He actually had surprisingly good taste for a jock, or at least had the sense to know he didn't, and take the suggestions of those who did.

The doorbell rang and he found Betsy on his front step, holding an eight week old, yellow Labrador retriever puppy.

"Holy Shnikeys, Shaggy.   This place is enormous!   Do you get lost trying to find the bathroom?" she asked.

"Not really.   I mean, there are six of them, so whatever direction I walk in, I'm bound to hit one," he answered with a wink.

"Six?!!   Why on earth do you need six bathrooms?"

"I didn't build the house. I just live in it. Who's this?" he asked, pointing to the pup.

"Your new roommate.   I figured you might get lonely living in this big place all by yourself."

"Does he have a name?"

"Hobbs."

"As in Roy, the best there ever was in the game of baseball?" he asked excitedly.

"I was thinking more as in Calvin and...but whatever floats your boat."

He stepped aside to let them both enter. Hobbs raced side to side from room to room, before deciding to relieve himself at the foot of the staircase.

"Lovely. I'm going to need to put a mop in every room," Teddy groaned. "But thank you," he smiled as he scooped him up and found himself the recipient of dozens of dog kisses.

"You're welcome. By the way, Madame Menendes is not very happy with your decision to not help fund the student trip to Paris over spring break."

"Funding it is not the problem. I could have helped fund it. The issue is that with the economy the way it is, I didn't feel comfortable asking families to come up with the extra money it would take for the students to go on the trip."

"Isn't that for them to decide?"

"It is. But at the same time, I didn't want some students to not be able to afford it that wanted to go, or even worse, families that really couldn't afford it, to stretch themselves too thin because they felt as though they had to send their son or daughter."

"Decisions like that will not make you very popular." she smiled.

"Luckily for me, Principal is a selected position and not an elected position," he grinned.

"And they don't have to agree with me, but they do have to deal with me."

"Aren't you a clever smarty pants."

"Tell me something," Teddy asked, pointing to the high school age boy in the next yard over. "What do you know about my neighbor?"

The kid was flying a remote controlled airplane in the yard, weaving its way in and out of the trees overhead. He was a decent sized boy, looked like he could be an athlete, except he didn't dress like one. Stonewashed jeans. Black Pearl Jam concert t-shirt. A well-worn pair of what was at one time white, Converse Chuck Taylor's on his feet.

"Joey Buttons?"

"Yes."

"He's a loner type. Quiet, but a decent sense of humor when you get to know him."

"Who does he hang out with?" Teddy asked.

"Well, by definition, loners tend to hang out by themselves," she answered with a smirk.

"Right," he answered, completely missing her sarcasm as he drifted off in thought. He hadn't left what was arguably the best job in college athletics to be a high school principal so he could fight with a French teacher. He had done it because he wanted to have more of an impact on the formative years of teenagers and here was his chance to do so.

It was time to get to work.

XIV NICK MORETTI'S BODYGUARD

Teddy arrived at school earlier than normal the next morning. He unlocked the doors and gates and turned on all the lights before retreating to his office for some interesting reading concerning one, Joseph Buttons.

Joey had accumulated sixty-four tardies in his four years at Bishop Martin, which had resulted in ten after school detentions and three in school suspensions. And yet, in the very definition of irony, he had never missed a day of school. Not one. He had no disciplinary record to speak of. No problems drinking, smoking or fighting. No disruptive behavior in class.

His GPA hovered just over a 2.0, but his SAT score was a 1270 for the two parts, which told Teddy that Joey was either extremely lazy or he had someone take the test for him. He tended to doubt he cared enough to do the latter, given his lack of effort in the classroom. He didn't play any sports, wasn't a member of the drama club, math league or any other extracurricular activity. But he did win 3rd prize in the Science Fair in 9th grade.

His report card comments said all you needed

to know about Joey Buttons. "Personable and a pleasure to have in class." "Bright, but lacks motivation." "Low test scores and missing assignments." "Fails to live up to his potential."

Teddy waited for the homeroom announcements to end before having Joseph Buttons called down to the principal's office. He could hear the collective "ooooohhh" from the students in the classrooms up and down the hallway.

A few minutes later, Joey knocked on his door and stuck his head in with a quizzical expression. "Hey, Chief. You rang?" The tone was more easy going than disrespectful.

"I hear 'Chief' and look around for the Lone Ranger and Tonto," Teddy replied.

"Who?"

"Never mind," he answered, frustrated at showing his age. "Have a seat."

"Am I in trouble?" Joey asked.

"Yes and no."

"I wasn't even late today."

"Well, I wouldn't brag too much about that considering you are in the process of setting a new four year record for tardies."

"I'm not following you."

"It's a victimless crime, or a self inflicted crime I should say. You have a 1270 SAT, but only a 2.1 GPA."

"Yeah, studying doesn't really do it for me," Joey answered.

"No one enjoys it, but you need your diploma

if you have designs on going to college."

"No designs on that, trust me. I'm planning to go into the Air Force."

"Why not go into an ROTC program at a college and become an officer?"

"College isn't for me. I'm more of an ideas guy."

Teddy choked on his cup of coffee.

"Did I say something funny?" Joey asked.

"No," he said slowly, gathering his composure. "You just reminded me of someone. So tell me, what do you do when you're not studying?"

"Not study," he responded with a wink.

"Near as I can tell you don't do much of anything else. Why don't we get you involved in an extracurricular activity?"

"Why?"

"Because don't you want to look back at high school and feel as though you were a part of something?"

Joey shrugged. It didn't seem to matter much to him.

"Ok, you might not care right now," Teddy admitted, "but trust me someday you will. And in the meantime, you never know, you might make a friend or two."

"I've got friends."

"I didn't say you didn't, but there's no such thing as having too many friends. Haven't you ever watched *It's a Wonderful Life*?"

"Yeah yeah. Ok, so what club or activity could I join?"

"How about one of the sports teams?"

"I'm not all that athletic. I can't catch a cold."

"What are you good at athletically?"

"I don't know. I can run a bit. And I like to hit things. Got a sport that utilizes those skills?"

"Well, assault and running from the cops isn't very sporting, but what about football?"

"They've already started haven't they?"

"Yes, but they're always looking for more bodies. Let me talk to Coach Kaplanis."

"I like the idea of hitting things, but I don't know."

"Think about it at least," Teddy pleaded.

"Fine. I'll think about it."

"And do me a favor. While you're thinking about it, open a textbook and study once in a while. You might actually learn something."

"You have my word I will do just enough to graduate on time," Joey answered with a smile.

Teddy shook his head and shook Joey's hand. It was difficult not to like the kid. Turning to his secretary once Joey turned down the hallway, he said, "Can you have Nick Moretti sent down to my office?"

Nick was the quarterback and Captain of the football team and arguably the most popular student in the school. He was smart, charming, friendly and wise beyond his years, most likely because he had been raised by a single mother and had independence forced upon him at a young age after he lost his father to cancer.

Nick was a good athlete, although not an elite

one, whose college career would likely either have to be at the Division III level or as a walk on in Division I. There was no concern about him making the adjustment from being the big man on campus to just another student, because sports did not define him. He was the Student Body President, President of the Varsity Club, a member of the Debate Club, a Mathlete, and even played a little guitar in the jazz band when time permitted.

"You wanted to see me, Mr. Kerrigan?" Nick asked.

"I did. I did. How are things looking for Friday night?"

"We're a little beat up on the O Line right now, so it could be a tough one. Xavier is also known for taking some cheap shots..."

"Then make sure to check your blindside and make quick decisions."

"I will."

"And how's your mom?" Teddy asked.

"She's good."

"Still working at the pharmacy?"

"Yeah. Night shift three nights a week. Pays time and a half though so she's happy about that."

"Well, give her my best," Teddy said, before getting to the real reason he had called him down. "So listen, I've got a favor to ask."

"Sure. What is it?"

"What do you know about Joey Buttons?" Teddy asked.

"Nice enough guy. Kind of keeps to himself.

Pretty smart, but never does his homework, so his grades aren't great."

"Who does he hang out with?"

"No one really. Not that I know of anyway," Nick answered.

"Doesn't go to parties?"

"Not any that I recall."

"Because he wasn't invited? Or because he didn't want to?"

"Maybe they didn't invite him because they didn't think he'd want to?" Nick reasoned.

"Ok, well, here's the favor. I want you to be nice to the kid. Become friends with him. I'm going to get him on the football team."

"What position does he play?"

"He doesn't. But he's a good sized kid who can run a bit and likes to hit people. Maybe he can help solve some of your O Line problems."

"Ok."

"Just pal around with him a bit. Make him feel comfortable. Invite him to a party or two. I think it would be good for him to be involved in something other than flying his remote control airplane," Teddy said.

"No problem."

Nick was an agreeable kid.

Teddy convinced Coach Kaplanis that adding Joey couldn't hurt and might even help, and enlisted Nick to convince Joey to come. Neither was sure he would show up. Until he did.

"We are a little light on the O Line, so that's where we are going to work you out," Kaplanis informed Joey.

"The O Line?   I have no idea what that means, but it sounds pornographic," Joey wondered aloud as several teammates roared.

Kaplanis glared at Teddy, who openly winced. Nick jumped on the sword.

"In a nutshell," Nick explained, "all you need to do is make sure, those guys don't get to the guy wearing the red pinnie, which in this case, is me."

"Are there any rules?" Joey asked, hoping against hope there weren't, but guessing there were.

"You can't grab them with your hands," Kaplanis interjected.   "You can't touch them outside the armpit area--"

"Why would I want to go near someone's armpits?" Joey cringed.

"You wouldn't. And you can't even if you wanted to. What you can do is push with an open palm with your hands in tight. Like this."

Kaplanis demonstrated on one of the defensive linemen and sent him flying backwards. He was in his fifties, but no one would have messed with him. "Or you can use your shoulder to knock them off balance if they're moving. As long as you get them in the chest. He showed what he meant on an unsuspecting player.

"Give it a try," he said to Joey. "Get in your stance first. Just like we showed you before."

Joey looked the part in his stance, but when the ball was snapped, the lineman on the other side just ran right past him.

"How am I supposed to stop him if I can't grab him?" a frustrated Joey asked.

"By your positioning. Their objective is to get to Nick, so if they go outside, eventually they have to come back in. Open up your stance and pivot so you're ready when they do," Kaplanis answered.

The next snap, Joey opened up and shoved the penetrating lineman so hard, he pancaked him into the ground.

He jumped up. "Is that allowed?" he asked.

"That's more than allowed. That's encouraged," Kaplanis laughed.

The following snap, two defensive linemen switched and both ran past Joey.

"What do I do when they do that?!" Joey asked.

"Pick up the inside rusher. Like I said, always easier if you keep them wide. But blocking schemes are complicated. You'll pick it up as you go. Best thing to do is watch the others in game situations. The game is the best teacher."

Kaplanis was being uncharacteristically patient. Besides, he had no intention of playing him any time soon. But sometimes, the best laid plains change.

Friday night was a war and Nick had already endured several late hits. When two Xavier players "high-lowed" him--meaning, one hit him low, while the other drove through him high-- Kaplanis had seen enough.

"Buttons!" he screamed.

Joey jogged over, helmet in hand. That was the first rule of football, Nick had told him. Always have your helmet with you.

"You remember everything we talked about in practice this week?" Kaplanis barked.

"Yes," Joey answered.

"Well, forget all of it. I want you go in there, and any player that crosses that line of scrimmage and moves toward Nick, I want you to flatten him. I don't care how you do it. And if Nick runs upfield, I want you as his bodyguard. Anyone tries to cheap shot him again after the play, bury him."

"Any way I want?" Joey smiled.

"Any way you want," Kaplanis repeated. "Send a message."

The words were still floating in the air when Joey sprinted onto the field and joined the huddle.

"81 fake reverse, naked bootleg on 3," Nick called out. "Joey, you better be ready because I'm coming right up your ass and I expect you to clear out a path wide enough for a dump truck to fit through."

"Well, if you remove the sexual overtones from your statement, I will do exactly that," Joey answered.

The ball was snapped, Nick faked the handoff to his wide receiver coming around and spun the opposite way. The first person Joey came in contact with was sent five yards backward with a completely legal block. The second was knocked even further and Nick shot through the hole. Twenty-five yards later, he jogged out of bounds up field with a first down and tossed the ball to the referee.   One of the Xavier players, however, didn't care that the play was over and began zeroing in on the unsuspecting quarterback. He never got there. Joey lowered his shoulder into the kid's chest and sent him flying into three teammates on the Xavier sideline, knocking them all over like bowling pins. The crowd went wild, and Nick Moretti had a new best friend.

XV   THE PROM KING

Teddy leaned back in his poolside recliner while Betsy swam laps on a sunny Saturday afternoon. Van Morrison played in the background. He had just about dozed off when he heard the click of the gate opening and closing. Nick Moretti and Joey Buttons entered the pool area.

"No room at the inn," Teddy said without looking up.

"Sure is hot out, Special K," Joey said, fishing around for a swimming invite. Seeing as they were already in their swim trunks, they weren't asking as much as informing him of their intent.

"That's what sprinklers are for," Teddy answered.

"Don't be an ass," Betsy said as she toweled off. "Let the boys go for a swim."

"What's in it for me? Ok, tell you what. You wash my car, you can use the pool."

"Your car has never had a spec of dirt on it," Nick said.

"Good point. Then how about you cut my lawn first?" Teddy asked.

"Your landscapers cut it yesterday."

"Another good point."

"I'm going inside to get some lemonade," Betsy said. "Anyone else want some?"

"I'd love some, Miss H. And here's what we will do for you, Special K. We will trade you some good advice for pool time," Joey said as he jumped in the pool cannonball style. Nick followed suit.

"Advice from you guys? Now that's rich," Teddy laughed.

Joey rested his arms on the side of the pool deck. "Yup. And here it is. You better ask Miss H to marry you before she smartens up and leaves your grumpy ass."

"We've only been dating for six months!" Teddy exclaimed.

"At your age, six months is like ten years," Joey answered.

"How old do you think I am?!"

"I don't know. Like 90?"

"I'm only forty!"

"Same thing."

And it was at that very moment that reality hit home for Teddy. Even though Joey was being sarcastic, the hard truth was that to teenagers, there was no difference between a forty year old and a ninety year old. Everyone over thirty was the same age to them.

"Do you love her?" Nick asked.

"I don't know. Maybe."

"Maybe?? Well, is she the last person you

think of every night before falling asleep?"

"That honor would belong to whomever is hosting SportsCenter because that is the last thing I watch before falling asleep," Teddy responded.

"Boy, how has no one snapped you up before now?" Joey remarked. "You're such a catch!"

"You guys are in love," Nick interjected. "You become Mr. Nice Guy every time she walks into the room. And she has a brain freeze every time you walk out."

"Brain freeze?" Teddy asked, sitting up now.

"Yeah. You can't ask her a question for like ten seconds after you leave a room because she's in fantasy land."

"All right. Let's say I took your terrible advice. How should I go about asking?"

"Just be yourself," Nick said.

Joey was floating in a chair in the pool now. "Actually, *don't* be yourself if you want her to say yes. And don't ask her on the scoreboard at Citi Field or anything cheesy like that."

"Don't be myself and don't be cheesy. That's your advice?" Teddy asked.

"Yup," Joey said as he flipped backwards and began doing the backstroke across the pool.

What Teddy didn't mention was that he had already bought a ring. He was just waiting for the right time to ask. That moment happened to be when they went for a walk on the beach one afternoon. Hobbs was darting in and out of the water as the waves crashed in around him, and as he watched Betsy's amused expression, he knew that she was the one above all others for him. Smart. Funny. Sweet. Inherently kind. He dropped to one knee and placed the ring box on the raised knee. She didn't even wait for him to ask--much less open the box to see the ring-- before saying yes and hugging him tightly. She looked like the girl asked to the prom by the prom king. She just had to wait 22 years for it to happen.

XVI NICK MORETTI GOES TO COLLEGE

Hot, dry and dusty was the best way to describe Indiana in early August. The fact that football players had to be on campus four weeks before everyone else made it somewhat depressing. There was no social life to speak of, in part because practices, mandatory meals and film sessions left little time for much else, but also because who wanted to get hit by a two-hundred and fifty pound locomotive with the acceleration of a Maserati when hangover?

Nick Moretti was the 4th string walk on quarterback at Notre Dame, which meant other than pre-game warm ups and the Blue-Gold game in the spring, he was as unlikely to step on the field at Notre Dame Stadium in an actual game as a reality TV star was of getting elected President. But it didn't make him any less important to the team. On the field, he was like having an additional coach, his keen understanding of the game offsetting any physical limitations he might have had at that level. Ironically, he could have gone to a number of places and been a star; just not there. He was ok with that though, because he loved the school, his teammates and his coaches. They felt the same way about him on and off the field. It also wouldn't have been a stretch to say that their All American quarterback would not have had nearly as much success had Nick not been there to push him, and it's safe to say, a number of the players on the team would not have had as much success in the classroom had Nick not been there to take notes and tutor them.

"Mr. Baronski," the professor bellowed towards an offensive lineman-looking fellow who had nodded off, "What does it mean to live in a PC society?"

Nick elbowed Baronski awake with a firm shot to the ribs.

"I'm sorry Professor Shapiro, I didn't quite get that," a groggy Baronski finally responded.

"I asked what it was like to live in a PC world," Shapiro repeated.

"I think it's great," Baronski said. "I don't know what people used to do before we had personal computers."

Nick winced in anticipation of the response from his crusty, jaded professor.

"Your answer, would in fact, be great, if we were in a Computer Science class," Shapiro stated, "but seeing as we are studying the US Constitution, it falls a bit short in the accuracy column."

Nick leaned in and whispered something to Baronski.

"Mr. Moretti. Are you Mr. Baronski's legal council?"

"I am, in fact," Nick responded. "And my client would like to invoke his Fifth Amendment rights."

"Very well. Although I might need to exercise my 28th Amendment rights."

"I thought there were only 27 Amendments?" Nick smiled.

"It's a little known one that hasn't yet been ratified that allows me to fail any student who falls asleep in my class," Shapiro smirked.

"I'll have to read up on that one."

"You should. But in the meantime, as the legal representative of the football program, how would you answer my original question?"

"What is it like to live in a PC society? I think it's kind of sad actually."

"How so?" Shapiro asked, intrigued.

"Instead of having discussions about whether and why people find some things offensive, we simply eliminate them altogether."

"An interesting point. How about if I invited Mr. Jones here over for dinner and served fried chicken with watermelon? Would you be offended, Mr. Jones?"

"I wouldn't be offended because I like both of those things," the African American young man in the front row responded.

"But what if you didn't?"

"I guess I would need to know the intent."

"Ahh, yes, intent. But how can we ever know

the intent for certain?" Shapiro asked.

"You can't," Nick interjected. "And that is the problem. People always assume bad intent, but shouldn't it be the other way around?"

"Assume good intentions unless proven otherwise?"

"Exactly."

"But that is not how society works," Shapiro continued. "People are easily offended. For example, sports team names are constantly protested and changed."

"In my opinion, that's ridiculous," Nick said. "My old high school used to be the Braves, but people protested so they are now the Wolves. How is Braves offensive? The very definition of the word means courageous and heroic."

"Ok, but what about Redskins?" a girl two rows in front of Nick interjected. He hadn't noticed her until she spoke, but suddenly couldn't take his eyes off of her. She was a petite brunette with flawless skin and bold blue eyes that looked even larger when seen through her sport framed glasses.

"What about it?" Professor Shapiro asked.

"The name refers to a time when Native Americans were killed, scalped and sold for their *red skins*."

"Mr. Moretti?"

"Being offended at that makes sense to me. Terms that most would find offensive shouldn't be tolerated. But I also think people need to not look for reasons to be offended. For example, we go to Notre Dame, home of the Fighting Irish. If you asked someone what that image represents to them, most would likely say a fighting, drunken Irishman, but you never hear Irish people complaining about that."

"Miss Doyle? I'm going to make an assumption here that you're Irish," Shapiro said to the brunette in the sport-rimmed glasses.

"Yes."

"And do you find our school nickname offensive?"

"I guess I hadn't really thought about it in those terms."

"So tolerance and good sense need to prevail," Shapiro summarized.

"If some school or pro team wants to call itself the Slippery Greeks, I'm ok with it," a boy near the back of the room offered.

"I'm sure they'd be grateful for your support, Mr. Panagiotidis. "But that brings up another issue. Stereotypes."

"Someone once said that stereotypes were formed because they are based in part on facts. Problems arise because even though a stereotype might be true for the majority, no stereotype covers everyone," Nick answered.

"And what person said that?" Shapiro asked.

"That would be you, sir. In your book."

"Ahhh, a football player who reads..."

"That would be an example of an offensive stereotype, sir," Nick smiled.

"Maybe one day we could break bread and

drink a little grappa along with our spaghetti and meatballs," Shapiro said.

"Most definitely, sir. Although I'm going to assume you'll want me to pick up the bill, Professor Shapiro," Nick answered as the class roared.

"An excellently offensive stereotype, Mr. Moretti," Shapiro responded before adding, "I think we are going to get along just fine this semester you and I."

The bell rang and Nick had only one thing on his mind. Catch up to the brunette in the glasses. Unfortunately, he caught up to her before he had figured out what to say.

He was walking alongside her for several steps in silence before she asked, "Can I help you?"

"I apologize for staring and apologize in advance if I offend you by saying this, but you might just be the most beautiful girl I've ever laid eyes on."

"I find that difficult to believe," she answered.

"Why is that?"

"Because I've been in your class for a month and this is the first time you've spoken to me."

"The world is full of magic things, patiently waiting for our senses to grow sharper. William Butler Yeats," Nick responded.

She blushed a deep Crimson and was unable to hold back a smile that was equal competition for her eyes on the beauty scale. "I have to go to another class," she said. "But thank you."

"Can I walk you there?" he asked.

"You just did," she answered as she turned toward the building next to them.

"Then can I marry you?" he blurted out.

"Why don't we start with lunch at the student center after this class?" she smiled.

"Deal. Do you have a first name?" Nick asked. "Or should I just call you Miss Doyle?"

"Diana."

"I'm Nick. And I'll see you in an hour."

He actually was supposed to watch film in an hour with the other quarterbacks and coaching staff, but they would all understand. Ok, maybe they wouldn't, but he suddenly didn't care. Some things were just more important.

XVII   THE FIRST DATE

Nick always viewed a movie as a safe first date in part because it eliminated the awkward silences of many first dates while they got to know each other, but also because it enabled him to slowly inch closer to his date in the darkness of the theatre.

"Popcorn?" he asked as they entered the lobby.

"Sure."

"Butter?"

"In the middle and on top!" she answered excitedly.

"Junior Mints?"

"My favorite," she smiled.

They decided on seats about halfway down and on the left side of the middle section, right on the aisle. When it was over, Nick couldn't have told you the plot points if you gave him a summer full of sunny days, because he had spent the entire movie trying to inch closer to Diana. He started by placing his arm and elbow on the armrest between them until it was touching hers ever so slightly. If a girl wasn't interested, they would nearly always move their arm off the rest. But if they were....they'd leave it there. Diana's arm never moved.

He then inched his hand towards hers, trying his best to make it look like an accident when they touched. Both pretended it hadn't happened, although that became a bit harder to ignore when a couple of their fingers interlocked, and eventually, their entire hands. It had only taken an hour and a half for it to happen.

The credits began to roll and the lights came on, but neither Nick nor Diana moved an inch.

"So...." Nick said at last.

"Buttons," Diana responded.

"I beg your pardon?"

"Sew buttons," she said. "My mother always says that when I start a sentence with '*sooooo*'."

"Ahhhh. Whenever I start a thought and then say *'I forgot what I was just going to say'*, my mother always says *'must have been a lie'*."

"Our mothers are strange people," Diana laughed.

"Or wise beyond our comprehension," Nick smiled.

The parking garage was still nearly full as the mall was not yet closed and people continued to show up in droves for the late shows. They had walked a considerable distance before Diana finally said something.

"Do you even know where the car is?" she asked.

"I have no idea," Nick answered. "I was kind of

hoping you did."

"I didn't pay any attention, because I thought you knew. You're the one who drove!"

"Maybe someone stole it?" Nick tried.

"Yeah, because so many people are dying to steal a twelve year old Firebird that starts only occasionally," she laughed.

"It starts all the time, but sometimes you have to play with the distributor cap first. It's actually a good anti-theft deterrent. But your point is well taken. And I could make up some line about how I was distracted by your beauty, but the truth is, I never pay attention in parking garages. This isn't the first time it's happened."

They were both laughing now.

"I think it's just down this row," he said.

Twenty minutes later, they were still searching when security drove up in a golf cart.

"You two need some help?" the guard asked.

"No--" Nick began before being cut off by Diana.

"Yes!" she said emphatically, while climbing into the back of the cart. "We can't find our car."

"I know where it is. I'm just a little turned around."

"Are you sure it's on this side of the garage? Or is it on the B side?"

"There's a B side??!" Nick and Diana both exclaimed in unison.

Nick climbed in the cart as well and the guard drove them to the other side of the garage where his car stood like the cheese--alone. He gave the man a slightly embarrassed nod as he thanked him, and opened the door for Diana. Not one of his prouder moments. He hated looking stupid, but if you couldn't laugh at yourself...

They arrived back on campus fifteen minutes later and parked in the student lot next to the football stadium. It was quiet for a Thursday night. The freshmen must have all been studying for their Friday "Emil", the weekly quiz named for the professor, that was given to students in advanced Chemistry. Or maybe they were resting up for a road trip weekend. The football team was headed to Ann Arbor to play Michigan. Nick would be leaving in the afternoon with the team in a caravan of buses.

"Do you have to go back and study for Emil?" Nick asked.

"I studied earlier. I wasn't sure how late you were going to keep me out," she smiled.

"Hopefully, a little longer at least. You want to go for a walk?"

Hand in hand they strolled leisurely through the North Quad. It was a gorgeous night. The first signs of summer turning into fall as a warm day had faded into a cool, refreshing evening, where you didn't quite need a sweatshirt, but would have been comfortable if you wore one. They settled on the step of the Clarke Fountain, or as the students often referred to it, Stonehenge, for its similarities to the ancient structure in England.

"Do you know the etymology of Stonehenge?" Nick asked.

"Can't say that I do."

"In Old English it is derived from the words 'stan' which means stone, and 'hencen' which means hang. Suspended stones. Impressed?"

"Surprised," she smiled.

"I'm not just another pretty face. I have a plethora of useless information. If you ever end up on Who Wants to be a Millionaire and need a lifeline, I'm your man."

"I'll be sure to remember that."

"So tell me about yourself," Nick said. "Where are you from?"

"I live in the suburbs of Boston with my parents."

"And what do they do?"

"My mom is a doctor at Mass General. My dad owns a garage."

"He owns a garage??! And you couldn't find our car?"

"Not a parking garage, numnuts," she laughed. "A gas station. And since, I don't know much of anything about cars, I'll likely follow in my mom's footsteps."

"Numnuts? Numnuts?" he repeated.

"Yes!"

"You're probably a Pats fan too."

"Actually, I'm not. My dad loved Joe Namath so I grew up a Jets fan. It's torture living in Boston as a Jets fan.

"Seriously?"

"Yup."

"My dad LOVED Joe Namath too, he said. "Ok, so you're a Jets fan. Big Plus. Music?" Nick asked.

"All kinds. You will find everything from Public Enemy to Glenn Miller on my IPod."

"Our freedom of speech is freedom of death, we got to fight the powers that be! Chuck D, in addition to having the deepest, most powerful voice, was one of the great lyricists and social commentators of our time. And Glenn Miller. It's impossible to not dance to In the Mood. Favorite movie?"

"Jerry Maguire," she answered.

"Jerry MaFuckingquire!"

"I know. I know. I can't help it. I like chick flicks."

"I'm not making fun of you. It's one of my favorites as well. Yes, it's a romance, but I love that it's about friendship and loyalty. I hate those stupid Hollywood critic type movies where everyone dies and the critics say how wonderfully creative it was. What's creative about that? Life can be depressing enough. I sure don't need to slap down ten bucks to see it."

"I agree 1000%. So what about you? Where are you from?"

"Born and raised in Connecticut. A little beach town named Milford."

Diana paused for a minute. "I know you will find this hard to believe, but I was born in Milford."

"You're playing with me, right?"

"I'm serious. We moved to Boston for my mom's work when I was five. So what do your parents do?"

"It's just my mom. My dad died when I was three. Cancer. I wish I could have known him or even remember him, because I heard he was an amazing guy. The day he died he saved a little girl who had fallen onto the train tracks. He died that night."

The color was flushed out of Diana's face and tears began streaming down as if someone had turned on a faucet.

"Did I say something--" Nick began.

She covered her face and began sobbing uncontrollably. He reached out to console her, puzzled though he was, but she stood up and began running for the dorm. He ran after her instinctively and caught her at the entrance.

"I....I....I'm so sorry," she wailed as she went inside and shut the heavy wooden door in front of him.

In a matter of seconds, what would have gone down as one of the best nights of Nick's young life, had collapsed into a confusing agony he simply didn't understand. He walked aimlessly around the campus by himself for nearly two hours, visiting places he didn't even know existed. At a little after one in the morning, he returned to his dorm. The student on duty nodded with his head in the direction of the lounge where Diana was sitting. The tears had been replaced by nervousness as he approached her.

"Did I say something wrong?" Nick asked once again.

"No. You didn't. Not at all," she answered.

"Then what happened?"

"You know how I told you I was born in Milford?"

"Yes. You weren't?"

"No, I was. This is difficult. When I was three, my parents and I were going into New York City for the tree lighting ceremony. I don't remember any of it of course, because I was too young, but my mom told me that I was walking along the platform at the train station and lost my balance. I fell onto the tracks just as a train was coming through. A man saw me fall, jumped down, grabbed me, hoisted me back onto the platform, and climbed back up himself just before the train roared past. That man, was your father."

Nick stood in silence for a longer time than perhaps Diana was comfortable with, his face betraying nothing, before a warm grin slowly spread across it.

"Well, that's an even better reason to love the man. He couldn't have left me with a better gift," he said at last.

Diana's emotions got the better of her again, and the tears flowed freely, but this time tears of joy. She ran into his arms and they kissed, not a normal, gentle, first date kiss, but one with all the passion and emotion of two people who came seconds away from never meeting; saved by a man neither of them remembered, but would both love forever.

XVIII MARRYING BETSY BLUES

After a year of planning in which Teddy's contribution consisted of dessert and wine tasting, he and Betsy were married in an outdoor wedding at a vineyard in northern Connecticut. Stonington was a picturesque little borough a few minutes south of Mystic, whose population was a mix of summer residents, retired former bankers, and wealthy wives interested in town gossip and flirting with their kid's soccer coaches while their husbands were away. But for a night anyway, a more eclectic collection of people that made up the motion picture of Teddy's life descended on Stonington.

Teddy went to elementary school with Marty Birmingham and had reunited over Facebook some years later, followed by dinners whenever Teddy was in town, or when Marty had come to South Bend. He was the President of a successful local bank in Connecticut and a lifelong Notre Dame fan.

"Back in 3rd grade, this fucking guy used to leap over the seats on the bus like a pommel horse in the Olympics," Marty bellowed to Betsy. She loved hearing what Teddy was like as a little kid before she knew him, and Marty had such an oversized, lovable personality, that you couldn't help be drawn to him. It didn't matter what he said. It was how he said it.

Tony Marini was an offensive and defensive lineman on Teddy's state championship team at Bishop Martin. He was a little undersized, but everyone was afraid of him nonetheless, because he wasn't afraid of anyone. His job was to keep Teddy upright and he would do whatever it took to do that. Tony went to college in Massachusetts and settled in the Boston area where he opened a "refrigeration" business with his Uncle Enzo, who mysteriously disappeared one afternoon in broad daylight. As the only son among his father and Enzo, Tony inherited the family business.

"Remember the party at Tommy's house when his parents were away and about 2,000 people showed up? Then I started a fight with half the football team from Fairfield Warde after one of them grabbed Betsy's ass?"

"You started that fight over *me*?!" Betsy exclaimed. She had always found Tony to be a bit rough around the edges in high school and had never been particularly fond of him, but she looked at him in a different light now.

"I told the guy to apologize and when he didn't, I dropped him. Then half the team jumped in behind him and none of my other pussy teammates helped except for Teduardo.

Just as a guy was about to cold cock me from behind, Teduardo smashed a chair over his head and it was on!"

"How did you guys not get arrested when the cops came?" Betsy asked.

"One of them knew my father and looked the other way, while we took off in a waiting car."

Teddy smiled sheepishly at the memory. Loyalty had always trumped stupidity in his life and Tony had never forgotten it.

"Teduardo?" Betsy smiled.

"We used to say he was Brown Irish because he had moves in the pocket like a salsa dancer and was smooth with the ladies."

Also in attendance that night was Tom O'Hara, the Heisman Trophy winning quarterback for the 1983 National Championship winning Notre Dame team. Tom was now on his way to the professional football Hall of Fame in Canton, Ohio as he neared the end of a spectacular career with the New York Jets. O'Hara had matinee idol good looks, which was handy since he was rarely seen not in the company of a movie star or super model. He was beyond rich and mobbed wherever he went in any of the seven different continents, equally famous for his athletic prowess, his choice of girlfriends, and from having schlepped on TV nearly every disposable and non-disposable item for sale in the US and abroad. If you rode in it, ate it or wiped with it, chances are he promoted it.

Teddy was a junior when Tom entered Notre

Dame; Tom as the All American quarterback and Teddy the 3rd string quarterback turned kick returner and defensive back on that same national championship team.

"NASA was lighting," Tom told the swelling audience by the bar.

"NASA?" somebody asked.

"That was his nickname," Tom answered.

"Because he accelerated like a rocket?"

"No. Because compared to the rest of the football team, he was a rocket scientist."

"Are we talking about the same Teddy?" Betsy asked bemusedly.

"4.0 GPA in the classroom and the ability to read any defense in the country. He just had a bit of a noodle arm."

Teddy nodded in agreement with a smile.

"It's safe to say, I would not be where I am today without his help. I still call him to help me analyze film in preparation for big games. Teddy broke a punt 70 yards in the Fiesta Bowl, but most people forget about it because he was pushed out of bounds at the 1 and I carried it in for a touchdown on the next play," Tom added.

After decades of constantly having to answer questions about himself, his last game, and his girlfriends, Tom loved being able to talk about someone and something else. For a change, there were no TV cameras or reporters, just good people. And for Teddy, life after high school had been largely one of anonymity as he took a backseat to others more talented, more athletic and brighter than he was. He didn't feel sorry for himself--far from it actually--as he knew he was fortunate to have experienced life in the spotlight at all. But it was still nice to hear someone everyone else respected singing his praises. A college athletic director and high school principal only became visible when something went wrong.

"Special K, I never knew you were so big time!" Joey Buttons exclaimed.

"I don't know about big time..." Teddy answered.

"Played on a college national championship football team, friends with one of the best Pro quarterbacks of all time, and marrying Betsy Blues," Nick Moretti answered, "I'd say that's big time."

Nick and Diana Doyle had been dating for nine months and all signs pointed to a future together. They enjoyed each other's company. They rarely, if ever, fought. And they didn't battle the jealousy issues that other couples their age did. Some people said it was because they didn't care enough. They knew it was because they trusted each other more than enough.

Joey Buttons had entered the Air Force Special Ops two weeks after high school graduation. He was a little more than a year into Combat Control training, one of the most grueling forces in the United States military. He stood a little taller, and spoke with more conviction, but still had the same sense of humor. He and Nick had remained close, with weekly letters that would occasionally become monthly ones if Joey had been deployed on a mission.

They laughed and drank and sang like the old days that night. Some people raced out of the reception at their own weddings, eager to begin their new life, but as eager as Teddy and Betsy were to start their new adventure together, they weren't quite ready to leave the old one just yet. They drank with their friends until the wee hours of the morning, and Teddy enjoyed the company of his former students for what would be the last time all of them were together. Six months later, Joey flew a mission deep into Iraq and was never heard from again.

XIX A SOLIDER'S SEND OFF

When Nick heard the news that Joey's plane had disappeared deep into the Iraqi night, his first thought was that there was no possible way he didn't survive. His second was heaven help who encountered a pissed off Joey. But when the hours turned to days, the days to weeks and the weeks into months, reality began to set in.

Diana and Nick flew back to Connecticut for the service on an overcast, breezy day in late October--the kind of day that people should be buried on. Sunshine coming into the world and clouds and wind going out. Other than Joey's family, Teddy and Betsy Kerrigan, and a smattering of others, there weren't many in attendance and it disturbed him.

"I mean I get that most people are away at college and some might not have the means to come back, but I can't believe there aren't more people here," Nick said sadly.

"Listen," Diana responded, "you should feel good about yourselves because you were the ones who recognized how great Joey was. It's their loss if they didn't take the time to get to know him."

"I know but still..."

"Most funerals for people that die young are crowded with hundreds of people that have no idea why they're really there," Betsy chimed in, "and even if they do know, they forget about it the second they leave the cemetery. Look around you. There isn't a dry eye in the church. It is far better to be loved well by a few, than just liked by many."

Teddy was glad she had said that because until then he was feeling the same way as Nick. As if their efforts to get people to see what a great person Joey was had failed. It took a woman's perspective for them to realize they had actually succeeded where others failed.

The shotgun blasts from the military tribute shook Nick to the very core and at that moment forced him to reevaluate his life goals. He wanted to make a difference like his friend had. He wanted to stand for something, but didn't have the same fearlessness that had driven Joey to join the Air Force. Law School and politics were immediately cast aside as trivial in his mind, and he changed his major from Pre-Law to Criminal Justice. Two weeks after graduating from Notre Dame, Nick accepted a position with the Defense Intelligence Agency. After nearly two years of on the job training, he eventually was assigned to the Defense Cover Office. His responsibility was to oversee and manage the cover of international agents involved in espionage.

Nick was the only contact many of these

operatives had with the United States Government and his job was to know their whereabouts at all times, while being careful to not expose them at the same time. It meant he needed to create layers upon layers of security. He had four different phones, ten different emails and never drove the same way to the D.C. headquarters two days in a row.

He enjoyed his work, but at times felt as though he was living in a Tom Clancy novel with phone calls at all hours of the night, and needing to travel internationally on short notice. It would have been a relationship killer for nearly anyone except someone completing their residency in medical school, which Diana was doing at nearby Johns Hopkins. She had an even worse schedule than he did.

Both longed for the day when they would be able to enjoy each other's company on a regular basis, and they knew it would someday come. It was just difficult to see that as the plane he was on passed over the Ostankino and Federation Towers in preparation for landing at Sheremetyevo International Airport. Christmas in Moscow was cold, dark and lonely. He hoped the North Face he brought was warm enough.

XX   NED O'BRIEN

Bianca Doyle graduated from Harvard undergrad and Yale medical school before eventually becoming the youngest Head of Oncology at Massachusetts General Hospital in Boston. Her daughter, Diana, always knew her mother had an important job that involved long hours and saving lives, but never knew the extent of it until she went into work with her for the first time when she was 12.

She went on "rounds" with her mother in the cancer wing, meeting people that were dying a slow, often painful death. How they handled that experience varied from accepting to angry. Some put on a brave face for their family, with the put upon smile quickly vacating their face as soon as the last family member left the room. They had made the decision that they didn't want to be remembered in their final days as a withering, bitter person. But the doctors and nurses received no such brave demeanors. Most people treated them as if they themselves were to blame for the unfortunate circumstances. In reality, it actually made it easier for the doctors, because it enabled them to distance themselves. It would have been impossible to handle the constant emotion of losing patients if they added an attachment to each and every case. No human would be able to withstand that and doctors of oncology had the highest patient mortality rate of any specialty. But as was usually the case, there was one exception to the rule. Someone so charming and so disarming that they made it impossible to treat them as just another patient.

Ned O'Brien was 88 years young when he was wheeled into the oncology wing with a smile. In fact, the smile never left his face, with the possible exception of turning into a slight wince when forced to give blood. He had lived a life that was equal parts incredible and tragic at the same time. His business, which he started with a small loan from his father, was manufacturing table leg balancers for restaurants and offices. The item was a small piece of plastic that worked similar to folded cardboard when placed under the offending leg. It snapped onto the leg and unscrewed to lengthen to the appropriate length needed to balance the table. Simply and accurately named the "table balancer", it came in four different sizes, fit most standard table legs, and at a cost of only 99 cents to make, allowed for a 300% markup for profit. Still, at only $2.99 each, Ned's father wondered exactly how he would be able to make a living selling them.

"By selling a lot of them," was Ned's response. And sell a lot of them he did, to the tune of five million a year to restaurants, offices and households. By the time he retired and sold the business to one of his floor managers, he had accumulated a sizable fortune.

He met Alicia Polaski when he was 35, a waitress who helped him sell his first set of table balancers to the restaurant where she worked. They married and had been together at the time of her death for more than 50 years. They laughed together. Traveled together. Watched TV together. Did crossword puzzles together. They also had two wonderful children, a boy and a girl, and had the opportunity to not only see them grow up, but had the opportunity to see their children's children go from crawling to staggering to eventually walking, then running as they became real people. The O'Brien's spoiled them rotten.

Alicia's health took a turn for the worse when she was 80, and at the recommendation of her doctor, they moved to Palm Beach, Florida, with the idea that the warm weather would help. It was an adjustment at first being away from friends and family, but adjusting came easily to Ned and the kids visited frequently.

On Christmas Eve of 1995, tragedy struck as 216 people were killed when an airplane crashed into the Atlantic Ocean just east of Florida. On board that flight were Ned and Alicia's children and all of their grandchildren as they headed down to spend the holidays with them. They missed their original flight by two minutes. If they had only made one more light on the drive to the airport, they might have made it.

Ned took it hard, but his wife took it harder, feeling responsible that they had even been traveling down there to begin with. She never recovered from it mentally or physically and passed away less than a year later. The cause of death was listed as natural causes, but could have just as easily have been listed as a broken heart.

Ned returned to Boston after his wife passed to spend his remaining years in a familiar environment, but soon began to outlive most of his friends. The day they wheeled him into Massachusetts General was the most interaction he had with people in two years. Perhaps that's why he was smiling.

"Dr. Doyle, your daughter really is cute as a button," he said the first time he met Diana.

"What's that supposed to mean?" Diana asked accusingly.

"It means your cute and little. Don't be rude," her mother admonished. It was amazing how quickly Bianca was able to switch from doctor to mother mode.

"Puppies are cute. Why can't I be pretty?" Diana wailed.

"Well, obviously you're pretty," Ned said. "But cute is even better. It's the best compliment you can give a girl, because it means you're pretty AND have a great personality."

"Oh! Thank you," she smiled. There was not a shy bone in Diana's body and never had been.

The two of them became fast friends from that moment on. They played checkers, watched TV, and read books together. She pushed him down the hallways to get a change of scenery. When he took a nap, she did her homework. She insisted on visiting every single day and had her father drop her off after school.

"Don't you have homework to do?" he asked.

"I'll do it at the hospital."

"Mr. O'Brien needs his rest you know."

"Ned is dying, dad. And I don't want him to die alone."

Her father nodded. He was a kind man and it was a trait he had passed on to his daughter.

"Ned, can I ask you something?" Diana asked one day.

"Of course," he responded weakly. The chemotherapy had taken its toll on him.

"I don't mean to be rude, but if you lost your wife and your kids and your grandkids, how come you're always smiling?"

He chuckled. "Because I've had enough good fortune and happiness to last five lifetimes. And because I'm going to get to see them all again very soon," he added with a wink.

Then one day, after not having a single visitor other than Diana for weeks, an older gentleman about Ned's age showed up unannounced.

"How're you doing, old timer?" the man asked.

Ned had been asleep, but his eyes shot open at the recognition of the familiar voice. "Jimmy?"

he answered with a smile, always with a smile. "What are you doing here?"

"I'm in town visiting some relatives and heard you were here so I thought I'd stop by to see how you were. I must say, you look like 25 bucks."

Ned started laughing until it made him cough. "When's the last time we saw each other? Alicia's funeral?"

"Think so. So who's this young lady?" Jimmy asked, nodding in Diana's direction.

"This is Diana. She's been showing pity on an old dying man by spending time with me."

"It's not pity," she protested. "I like it."

"She is cute as a button!" Jimmy remarked.

"Isn't she?" Ned agreed.

"What is it with you guys and your cute as a button comment?? I don't see how buttons are even cute."

Jimmy helped his old friend into his wheelchair and took him on a stroll through the hospital, even getting permission to go outside so Ned could feel the warm summer breeze. They laughed about old times and for a while anyway, Ned forgot he was sick. He was exhausted by the time they returned to the room, but in a good way. Ned leaned back in his bed with a content smile on his face and fell asleep.

"Will you be coming by again tomorrow?" Diana asked Jimmy hopefully.

"I'm afraid not," he answered. "I live in California now and have to get back."

"Oh, I thought you were visiting family here."

Jimmy shook his head. "Our friend here is a special man. Years ago, when I lost my job, he paid my mortgage for me for nearly two years, but denied it was him. Made up some story about a veteran's fund he was able to tap into for me because he didn't want me to feel badly. Well, I didn't want him to feel badly about me traveling all the way here today, but the truth is, I came just to see him. I came to say goodbye."

Jimmy leaned forward and kissed Ned gently on the top of his head and Diana saw the tears welling up in his eyes, before they started streaming down his face. He wiped them away with the back of his hand and left the room, pausing in the doorway to look back at his friend one last time.

"Mom!" Diana screamed as she burst into her office. "Can't you give Ned something? An antidote or serum that will make him better?"

"I'm afraid not, sweetheart."

"I hate that he's suffering. One day, I'm going to find a cure for cancer. I promise you I will."

"I believe you," Bianca smiled.

"I don't want him to leave, but I also don't want him to suffer anymore either."

That night, Ned O'Brien closed his eyes one final time, and began the journey to rejoin his family.

XXI NED O'BRIEN'S MONEY

With no family or close friends left, a few days before he died, Ned O'Brien changed his will to leave everything to a certain 12 year old with a simple note attached.

"I have confidence when the time comes you will know what to do with this," the note said.

It was a huge responsibility for her to shoulder and she didn't touch a dime of it for 15 years, even though her mother and father told her Ned would have wanted her to enjoy some of it for herself. By the time she finished her residency at Johns Hopkins, the fortune had grown to more than 150 million dollars. After some soul searching, she finally knew what she needed to do and began to fund a laboratory for cancer research.

She spent 16 hour days for three years, even more when Nick was away, locked in her basement lab studying cultures of human cancer cells. It was cheaper than animal testing, more efficient and more humane. The most common cancer treatment involved chemotherapy, which involved killing cells the multiplied quickly, which was the most identifiable characteristic in cancer cells. The problem was that there were also "good" cells that multiplied quickly and that created horrific side effects.

Targeted chemotherapy treatment involved identifying what other characteristics separate a fast multiplying cancer cell, from a healthy fast multiplying cell in order to "target" the cancer cell and prevent it from growing. The problem was that there were a number of different types of cancers, many of which had distinctly different characteristics. Diana concluded that she needed to find the one characteristic they all shared.

After two years and seventeen days, she found out what it was. CD-47. It was a protective protein produced by cells that alerted white blood cells not to attack and kill them. The problem was that cancer cells produced CD-47 in large quantities. So Diana needed to create an antidote that would be injected directly into the bloodstream, identify cancer cells by the quantities of CD-47 they produced, and prevent them for making more. In the ideal world, over a period of days, the serum would stop the production of the protein in cancer cells, and allow the body's own immune system to kill off the offending cells, much in the way antibiotics worked.

On the 1,128[th] day of her research, she studied the culture of human cells that had received the injection five days earlier. She rubbed her eyes to make sure they weren't playing tricks on her, even wiped the microscope lenses clean, and looked again. She wasn't even sure why she was so surprised at what she saw, but she was. Much in the way a Super Bowl winning coach thought they could win the big game, but was stunned when it actually happened. In her mind, thousands of far better and smarter people than her had tried to find a cure for more than 3200 years and failed. It was a thought that plagued her for all of thirty seconds before she grabbed her cell phone and called a colleague.

"Are you in the building?" she asked when the person on the other end answered. "Get down here. Quick. Like run. I need to make sure I'm not seeing things."

The sound of the heavy footsteps on the tile floor could soon be heard, followed by the beeping of the lock code. A man entered. Mid-30's. Awkward. His glasses had slipped down his nose while he ran, so he pushed them up with his forefinger.

"What is it?" he asked.

Diana just smiled in response.

"No," he said.

She nodded.

"Noooo way!"

She nodded again and with a tilt of her head, "See for yourself."

The man looked in the microscope, then studied the computer screen in front of him. "And this is...."

"Sample C."

He looked again, almost in disbelief.

"I did the same thing," she said.

"Oh my god, Diana," the man said in near shock, "You've found a cure for cancer."

Her next step was to get in to see the Federal Drug Administration so they would allow her to do trial testing on humans with little hope. It took longer than she hoped to get an appointment, but she decided she didn't need one after all and showed up at their headquarters in Silver Springs, Maryland unannounced.

The Center for Drug Evaluation and Research was tasked with the job of determining which drugs were safe and effective before being introduced to the general public. They didn't perform the actual tests themselves, but rather evaluated the results and research of drug companies or companies sponsoring the research. Diana had performed her studies outside the spectrum of the traditional drug companies so that she wouldn't have to face the bureaucratic red tape on a daily basis that would limit her progress.

"I've found a cure for cancer," she blurted out to the FDA administrator.

"I beg your pardon?" the man asked. He was more suit than scientist. Dark, slick-backed hair with just enough grey as to look distinguished. Nicer suit than someone on his salary probably should have been wearing.

"I've found it," she reiterated.

"For what type?" he asked curiously.

"For all of them."

"Excuse me? How is that even possible?"

"Cancer cells produce CD-47, which is the protein that protects the cells from being attacked by the bodies own immune system."

"I'm aware of that."

"I've found a way to block those cells from producing the protein. Other people have found ways to block forming the protein as well, but it blocked production of the protein from healthy cells as well which left the immune system extremely weak. It would destroy itself. I've found a way to target only the cancer cells by recognizing the *amount* of CD-47 they produce."

The man did not react with the enthusiasm Diana had expected. He wrung his hands in front of him while she spoke. Then eventually stood and walked over to the window.

"That's fascinating," he finally responded. "I look forward to reading and studying your research."

"How long before I could potentially get permission for trial testing to begin?" Diana asked.

"Oh that could take a while," the man said. "Months. Maybe even a year or two."

"Excuse me?"

"Well, we have to review your studies. Then perform a few of our own. Not to mention have you run tests on animals before using it on humans."

"Animals have a different makeup. It is unlikely to have the same results on them. My thought would be to run trial testing on those people that are out of other options. That have nothing to lose."

"You don't even know what the potential side effects could be."

"No. But I can guess based on what happens when CD-47 production is stopped."

"We are not about guessing at the FDA."

"There won't be any side effects if I'm correct because my antidote will only stop the production of CD-47 in cancer cells and leave the others alone."

The man ran his hand over his chin in thought. "As I said, I'll study your results and get back to you in a few days with the next steps." He stood again and extended his hand. "I appreciate you coming by and of course, all the countless hours you have put into this."

Diana shook his hand but was puzzled. She hadn't expected a ticker tape parade, but she did expect a bit more enthusiasm. That would have to come from her husband. She called his cell phone, but it was midnight in the Middle East and it went straight to voice mail.

"Hi babe. I know it's kind of late there, but I miss you and miss hearing your voice. I've got some incredible news I want to share with you. Call me when you can."

She looked in her rear view mirror and noticed the same shaped headlights had been following her for a while. They were distinctive and large, like those on a Ford Explorer. She made three or four turns and the car stayed behind her at a safe distance. Eventually it turned off on its own and she breathed a sigh of relief. It had been nothing but her mind playing tricks on her, but she pulled straight into the garage, and turned on their alarm system, along with nearly every light in the house just to be safe. Eventually, she drifted off to sleep with thoughts of saving the world and Ned O'Brien being proud that she was using his money to help people.

XXII   THE ELIMINATION DEPARTMENT

The following morning, Diana rose early, showered, and made her way into the laboratory. What did you do the day after you found a cure for cancer that you weren't allowed to use yet? She wasn't sure, but decided to see if she could find more evidence to substantiate her claims that she could send over to the FDA.

She waved to the security guard at the front kiosk, and took the elevator to the basement. It was quiet down there, the way it always was. She punched in the code on the keypad and the light turned green. Diana entered, stopping in the doorway when she looked up. The entire lab had been trashed. Bottles broken. Microscopes and computer screens thrown to the floor and smashed. Her file cabinets had been ripped open and papers randomly thrown throughout the room. The security cameras on the ceiling had been painted over.

Whoever did it was obviously looking for something, but they weren't going to find it there. She didn't spend years and millions of dollars only to, as her father always warned her not to, "leave all her eggs in one basket". No, whoever did it walked away empty handed. But who was it? Only a select handful of people even knew what she was working on and one of them was in the Middle East. Then there was the question of how they got in there in the first place?

"Who was on duty last night?" she asked the guard at the front.

"Harold was on, but had already left when I came in," the man answered. "Which is strange because we're supposed to make sure there is no lapse in coverage."

"And does the night guard regularly perform rounds to make sure everything is ok?"

"Of course. Is everything all right, Dr. Doyle?"

The security cameras would undoubtedly show something. They filmed every person that entered the building, every corridor, every elevator, every staircase, every room. She could go one of two ways with this. Call the police and have Harold brought in for questioning. Or act as if nothing had happened. That would be something they wouldn't expect and would undoubtedly draw whoever did this back out into the open.

"Can I see the security footage from last night, Danny?" she asked.

"Sure," he responded before repeating, "Is everything all right?"

"Everything is fine. Someone played a little

joke on me and I just want to see if I can catch them in the act."

"Ohhhh," Danny smiled. He went into the other room and returned a minute or so later. "Umm, the security footage from last night is missing."

"What do you mean missing? Isn't it all computerized?"

"Yes. But the files have been deleted."

"Is that easy to do?" she asked.

"You'd either need to be a computer hacker or have someone in the know do it for you," Danny responded. "Want me to call Harold in?"

"Yes," Diana said unenthusiastically. Based on the facts that were unfolding so far, Harold had probably gone the way of the Dodo bird. He was likely extinct.

She wasn't sure what to do next. She was a doctor and a scientist, not an FBI agent. But then she flashed back to the night before when she thought a car was following her. Now, it made sense. They weren't following her home. They were making sure she wasn't going back to the lab. But it also meant they probably knew where she lived. She raced out the door without another word.

"Dr. Doyle?" Danny said, his voice trailing after her.

It was a little more than a 40 minute drive from campus to their house, but she was trying to make it in 20. Weaving in and out of traffic on the parkway, she was driving like a teenager racing one of their friends to a party. Diana skidded to a half stop off the exit ramp, before sliding into a sharp turn. She hit the gas to pull out of the fishtail and started down the narrow, two lane, wooded road that led to their house.

"Call. Nick," she spoke into the Bluetooth in her car.

The call went straight to voice mail. She checked her rear view mirror and saw a lone truck in the distance. She was going 80 and it was gaining on her. Diana looked ahead trying to navigate a sharp curve and when she checked her mirror again the truck was gone from view. It was now next to her. The black Ford Explorer side swiped her on the turn and sent her careening into the ravine below, bouncing from tree to tree like bumpers on a pinball machine, until her car finally came to an abrupt halt headfirst into a waiting 100 year old oak tree at the bottom.

Nick's phone started ringing the moment he turned it back on. He had been in the middle of an intel operation in which he needed to get one of their DIA agents out of Afghanistan. When Nick heard the voice of the police officer who had found his wife, he felt a sudden chill shoot down his spine. He hadn't slept in more than 24 hours and wouldn't sleep a minute on the eight hour flight back to Washington.

He arranged for a car to take him directly to the hospital where his wife lay conscious and breathing on her own, but badly bruised and harboring more than a few broken bones. She had been extremely fortunate.

"My god. Are you ok?" he gushed as he entered the room.

"I'm fine," she said.

"You look fine," he answered, shaking his head.

"Really, I am. It could have been a lot worse."

"What is going on? Your car gets run off the road. Armed guards in the hallway. I don't understand."

"You want the short or long version?" she asked.

"Short."

"I discovered a cure for cancer and now someone wants me dead because of it."

"Jesus. That was short. Why?"

"I have no idea."

"Who knows about your discovery?"

"My lab partner, Peter."

"I've met him. He's scared of his own shadow. Who else?"

"The FDA."

"The FDA?"

"Yes. I went there to apply for approval."

Nick sat in a chair next to the bed, and held her hand. "There's your answer."

"I don't understand."

"Who wouldn't want a cure for cancer?"

"I can't imagine anyone wouldn't."

"Think about it in terms of money. Who

would stand to lose the most if a relatively simple, inexpensive cure for cancer was found?"

"The drug companies," she groaned.

"Exactly. Look at the top producers of cancer treatment medication, and there's our suspect list."

Cache. Bethany-Peters. Novellis. Fairmont. Merced and Company. They were the top five oncology drug companies and accounted for more than 60 *billion* dollars in sales. People had killed for far less.

Nick knew where he needed to go to narrow down the list. Craig Coffey was the Deputy Director of the DIA and Nick's boss.

"I mean, what you say is certainly plausible. We are talking big money. *Big* money."

"I know our agency is more of an international operation and we aren't the FBI. But I thought maybe, you might know someone who could help. I don't know what to do. I don't know how to protect my wife."

"Well, technically, we are an international agency. But we do have a department very few people know about that focuses on national security and intelligence. Works closely with the NSA and FBI. What do you need them to do?"

"I need them to eliminate the problem," Nick said.

Craig nodded. In their line of work, elimination was sometimes a necessity of business. "I had a feeling you'd say that," he said, before adding after a pause, "There's a guy who could probably help. He's an expert at eliminating problems. I'll set it up."

Located in the basement of the far east wing of the DIA, the office of "elimination" was so secret that it didn't even have an official name. In fact, its indescript set up could have easily been confused with a furnace or maintenance room. Craig swiped his ID card for entrance and a man inside looked up suspiciously with a start.

"Is he in?" Craig asked.

The man nodded towards the back. Another man was seated with his back to the door. He turned slowly to face them and the color drained quickly from Nick's face. He was too stunned to utter a syllable.

"No fucking way," were the words that finally came out of his mouth when he found himself face to face with a dead man. Joey Buttons grinned an easy grin and winked at his old friend.

XXIII THE ELIMINATOR

Nick stared down his friend, running his hand over his own face, scratching it while he collected his thoughts.

"I was at your funeral," Nick said at last.

"So was I," Joey answered. "Just not in the casket."

"Does this mean you never were in the Air Force?"

"No, I was. And I did get shot down in Iraq. But they pulled me out. And when they did, they asked me to work for this new agency. Said my personality fit the profile. Whatever that meant. And what better person to work undercover than someone who is already dead?"

"And you couldn't let me know you were alive?"

"I couldn't let anyone know. You know the drill. You work here. Do you let your current undercover agents contact past friends or family?"

Nick nodded understandingly. It was the most difficult part of the job.

"So why is it ok now?" he asked.

"Truthfully?"

"No. Lie to me," Nick said sarcastically.

"I had no idea it was you when Craig called down. He just said one of our own needed help. Said it was life or death. And so here we are."

"So Diana--"

"The girl from the wedding?" Joey interrupted. "You married her?"

Nick nodded. "Seven years now."

"No shit. Anyway, sorry. Continue."

"She's a doctor. A research scientist actually. Self funded. She was left this money by this old guy when she was 12," Nick explained.

"That sounds a bit West Virginiaish," Joey said.

"It's not like that, but it is a long story. And it was a shitload of money. So she's funded her own research into cancer. Most scientists are sponsored by drug companies. The problem with that is that they always place restrictions on you. Limit your funding and you have to go through so much red tape to get more of it that it makes it difficult to accomplish much. After seeing how it works, it's no surprise to me that they haven't found a cure. Anyway, after several years, Diana found one."

"Found what? A cure?"

"Yes."

"Only you would marry the person who cured cancer. And the world's longest winning streak continues," Joey laughed.

"This happened this past week while I was away. And since then, her lab was destroyed, her car was forced off the road and someone broke into our house."

"Someone's looking for her notes. Could be because they want to duplicate them and sell the cure to a drug company for themselves. But more likely, it's one of the drug companies not wanting the cure to go mainstream. Follow the money."

"That was my thought too. The companies would stand to make a lot more money with treatment drugs than a cure for it. There are other ripple effects as well. Without cancer, people would tend to live longer, which would then affect social security, which is already struggling."

"It's messed up is what it is. She has a chance to save millions upon millions of lives and they're thinking with their wallets," Joey said.

"So how do we find out who *they* are?"

"Leave that to me. In the meantime, where is Diana?"

"She's at Walter Reed. They were worried about internal bleeding and it was the closest hospital."

"Perfect. She's safer there than she'd be anywhere else," Joey said.

"But they're going to release her soon. Probably by this weekend."

"That creates more of a problem," Joey lamented, the wheels turning in his head. "Ok, here's what I need you to do. First, get anything of value in her research together and hide it in an unmarked storage unit. Make extra copies for yourselves."

"That's already been done. Diana is a planner. And slightly paranoid."

"Paranoid is good for something like this. Then what we need to do is hide her somewhere."

"But where?" Nick asked.

"Not around here. And not in Boston. That's where she's from, right?"

"Correct."

"That'll be the first place they look then. At her parents if they're still alive."

"They are," Nick responded. "Where then?"

Joey didn't answer right away. He was ten thoughts ahead already. "My parents," he said at last. "They'll never associate her with me and besides, I'm dead as far as anyone knows."

Nick nodded slowly in agreement. "Do your parents even know you're alive?"

"They do. I couldn't not tell them. But I've barely seen them or had much contact with them."

"But it was ok to let me think you were dead..." Nick replied.

"C'mon. They're my parents."

"The bigger question is how we stop the people that are after Diana?" Nick asked.

"Like I said, leave that part to me. Some things you're better off not knowing."

XXIV A SORT OF HOMECOMING

Three days later, Nick waited until dark to sneak his wife out of the back entrance of the hospital. She was able to walk, but was noticeably and understandably sore and weak. They made the five and a half hour drive to Connecticut, arriving just after midnight. Nick had been back only once since Teddy and Betsy's wedding 10 years ago. With his mother now living in South Carolina, and most of their friends living elsewhere, there wasn't much of a reason to.

The Buttons were waiting for them when they arrived, already in their pajamas, as they usually were on any night after 8:00pm. They hugged Nick and Diana as if they were their own flesh and blood.

"I'm sorry it's so late," Nick apologized. "We hit a little traffic on the GWB."

"It's not a problem. It is so good to see you. We rarely get to speak to Joey, much less see him. Having you here is like having a part of him here with us."

The Buttons showed them to the guest room, which, as often as Nick had been in their house as a teenager, he had never actually been in.

"If I can bring you anything else to make you more comfortable, dear, don't hesitate to ask," Mrs. Buttons said to Diana.

"This is perfect," Diana answered, a bit worn from the trip, but happy to be surrounded by people that were looking out for her.

She readied for bed and crawled under the comforter. With no beeping sounds from medicine dispensing machines, or groaning from suffering patients to distract her, Diana was asleep within minutes. Nick went downstairs to wait for Joey, who had texted to let him know he was a few hours behind them. He entered quietly at three in the morning, but Nick was still awake anyway. He hadn't slept much in the past week and it was starting to show. Joey nodded to follow him out to the back patio so they could talk without fear of waking anyone, while also enjoying the crisp fall evening.

"How was the drive?" Nick asked.

"Same as yours I imagine," Joey responded. "Long, dark, and surprisingly, full of traffic and construction on the George Washington Bridge."

"So is it done?" Nick blurted out, unable to make small talk any longer.

"It's done," Joey answered.

"It was Cache wasn't it?"

Joey nodded. "They have the highest volume of oncology medicine sales, and a far smaller volume of everything else. As I said, follow the money."

"I saw on the news tonight that their CEO died from a stroke," Nick said.

"Tragic."

"But how do you know that will solve the problem?"

"We eliminated the person who wanted to eliminate Diana. Problem solved. We also sent a rather unmistakable message to those next in command in the process."

"Thank you," Nick said quietly. They sat in silence for a few minutes before he added, "Can I ask you something?"

"Sure."

"Does it bother you?"

"Does what bother me?"

"Killing people."

"Oh. Well, technically, I didn't kill him. I just helped facilitate it."

"But does that bother you?"

"You want to know something strange? When I was in the Air Force and I flew bombing missions, we killed hundreds, but I didn't think much about it. I guess because I was so far removed from it. But when my plane went down, and I saw up close the destruction and deaths that we had caused, it really hit home. I mean, I had killed innocent people. Not intentionally, but that didn't make it right. So when they offered me a different opportunity, an opportunity to not kill indiscriminately. To not even do it myself. To plan it against bad people. People that deserved it. I looked at it as my chance at redemption. I know that sounds warped, but I justified it by thinking that killing bad people actually saved lives."

"It probably did. What kind of bad people?" Nick asked.

"Remember when they found Saddam Hussein in that underground shelter?"

"Of course. You planned that?"

"No. But I planned the capture of his nephew's second cousin twice removed by an arranged marriage."

Nick laughed out loud.

"Don't laugh," Joey said with a smile, "He was one bad dude. For a 16 year old."

"So what now?" Nick asked.

"I'm thinking it's time to find another line of work."

"Like what?"

"I don't know. Something completely opposite of what I do now. Maybe sales. Something that would force me to talk to people. I'm thirty years old and other than you, I've never had a friend."

"That's not true," Nick said, even though in his mind he knew it probably was.

"Sadly, it is."

"What about Special K?" Nick asked, pointing to the house next door.

As if on cue, Teddy Kerrigan emerged from his house and stood by the flagpole in his backyard. Although it was difficult to make out much more than his silhouette in the moonlight, he almost looked as if he was praying. When he finished, he turned and for a brief moment, appeared to be looking at them. Nick and Joey both waved, but Teddy didn't acknowledge them and continued into his house.

XXV   CONNER KERRIGAN

Nick and Joey rang the doorbell of their former high school principal's house around noon the following day. They weren't sure if he hadn't seen them the previous night, ignored them, or was simply distracted by something else. There was something decidedly different about the moments that followed. There was no barking dog, no screaming wife, no sound of a running pre-teen towards the door. Just when they had begun to walk away, the door was slowly pulled open. Teddy looked out suspiciously with at least a one week beard growth, wearing a t-shirt, jeans and a baseball cap pulled down low.

"Oh. Hey," he said distractedly as he stepped aside to let them in. He didn't give the slightest indication that he was even remotely surprised to see Joey alive.

"Thanks for blowing us off last night," Joey started.

"What are you talking about?" Teddy responded.

"Last night. You looked right at us in the backyard and we waved, but you showed us no love."

"I didn't see you," he said distractedly.

"Are you all right?" Joey asked. "You look like shit."

"As bad as I look, I feel even worse," he said. "C'mon in."

"What's wrong? You sick?" Nick asked.

"No. But my son is." Turning to Joey, he casually asked, "Didn't I go to your funeral?"

"As Twain once said, reports of my death were greatly exaggerated."

Teddy nodded. On a different day, he might have had a stronger reaction or had a follow up question, but not on this day.

"That's right," Nick said. "You have a son now. How old is he?"

"Conner is 9."

"What's he got? The flu?"

"I wish," Teddy said sadly. "He had been begging me to take him to his first Mets game for a year. So finally, in April, I pulled him out of school, called in sick myself, and took him to Opening Day."

"How'd he like it?" Joey asked.

"Loved it. Got the full experience. Train ride into Grand Central Station. Subway out to Citi Field. All the food he could eat. But on the way out of the stadium, he suddenly asked if he could have a minute to catch his breath. It was only about fifteen steps and normally he would have run up them two at a time. I thought maybe he was just worn out from a long day, but when it was worse the next morning, I took him to the doctor. They looked him over. Did some blood work and then called at like 11 o'clock that night and told us we needed to come in first thing in the morning." Teddy paused as if he could barely make himself utter the words, "He has acute leukemia."

"Jesus," Joey muttered.

"Oh my god. Is he going to be all right?" Nick asked.

"That's just it," Teddy said. "The doctors have said there's nothing else they can do for him. They're sending him home for his final days. Betsy is riding with him in the ambulance. I came back early to make sure the house was set."

"I don't know what to say," Nick responded.

"I'm so sorry, Special K," Joey added.

"He's a great kid. Smart. Funny. Good hearted. Loves all sports. Football. Baseball. Basketball. Soccer. Follows politics. Plays the drums. He could have been anything he wanted to be."

"He still can," Joey said.

"Didn't you hear me? The doctors already said there's nothing else they can do."

"Maybe they can't," Nick said, "But maybe we can."

XXVI   A LIFE IN THE BALANCE

Diana paced across the living room as Teddy and Betsy anxiously looked at her.

"The thing is this. It works, or at least it's worked in the extensive tests I've run. But I haven't tried it on blood cancers yet. Theoretically it should work the same way. The antidote identifies the cancer cells and blocks them from producing the protein that protects them from the body's immune system. It's similar to how antibiotics work. They stop a bacteria from growing and let your body take care of the rest."

"At this point," Betsy said, "we have nothing to lose. Our son has days, maybe a week to live. We are willing to try anything."

"It definitely works," Diana assured them. "I've tested it ten different ways to Sunday. My concern is whether or not it is too late. If his immune system is already too weak to fight back."

"Then let's not wait any longer to find out," Teddy insisted.

Diana nodded as she opened the small cooler in front of her. Within it, she removed a blue bottle holder. Unscrewing the bottom, she slid a tall, thin container out from inside.

"You've been keeping the cure to cancer in a coozie?" Joey asked.

"It's neoprene-lined; that along with the cooler and ice, kept it cold while we traveled. It's been in your parents' garage fridge since we got here."

He nodded as if that made sense, when in reality, not much had made sense over the past week or so.

"How long will it take to work?" Teddy asked.

"If it works," Diana said, trying to temper expectations, "we should start to see improvement within 24-48 hours. Just like with strep throat or a bacterial infection."

It was one thing to perform tests on cells. Another to perform them on a living creature or person. And yet another still to try it on the little boy of people your husband knows and loves. She took a deep breath and entered the bedroom alone, emerging a few minutes later.

"His vital signs are low, but stable. He's sleeping comfortably," she said when she returned.

"He's been sleeping virtually non-stop since coming home yesterday," Betsy responded.

"What now?" Teddy asked.

"Now we wait and monitor him," Diana answered.

"I'm going to sit with him in case he wakes up," Betsy said.

"I'll sit with you," Diana offered.

And the men stood alone. Helpless. Fearful. With the faintest glimmer of hope keeping them going.

"You know, when you think about it," Nick began, "it really is amazing that we are all here together today."

"How do you mean?" Teddy asked.

"Well, so many things had to happen. So many decisions were made that affected all of our lives without us even realizing it. For example, my father had cancer, and my mother told me at first he wasn't going to fight it. Wasn't going to receive treatment of any kind."

"Why not?"

"Didn't see the point I guess in extending his life by a few months only to feel lousy the entire time."

Teddy nodded. But that was a decision easier to make for yourself than someone else.

"But then a friend of his from high school, who he thought had died a couple of years earlier, showed up and talked him into fighting it. His friend had faced a similar decision apparently and made a similar choice as my dad, but was saved when an organ donor appeared at the last minute. A few more days and Philip Halmer wouldn't have been there to talk my father into fighting for his life. And if he hadn't fought for it, I probably wouldn't be here today. My dad lived an extra three years he wouldn't have otherwise. Diana's story is even crazier," Nick continued.

"We have nothing but time," Joey offered.

"Well, Diana's mother is a doctor as well. She's the Head on Oncology at Mass General up in Boston. But when she was younger, she did her residency at Yale. Which is where Diana was born. Crazy thing is, Diana's parents almost never met."

"How come?"

"Diana's mom never took any time off. Like never. Still doesn't. But her favorite band growing up was Running Water."

"I remember them," Teddy said. "Where Would I Be Without You."

"That was her favorite song. Anyway, the band was doing a reunion concert with Depeche Mode at the Oakdale up in Wallingford so she took the evening off. But on their way to the show, the band's bus slipped off the road and went into a ditch. Everyone lived, but the lead singer was in pretty rough shape. They brought him to Yale and she was the one who operated on him. Saved his life."

"That's really cool," Joey said.

"It gets better. Obviously, without the lead singer, they were going to cancel the show, but who shows up at the hospital that day? The former lead singer. And he offers to help them out by performing with them for that night because he knew financially the band was in trouble and needed the money. It would be like David Lee Roth showing up at the hospital after Sammy Hagar got in an accident and agreeing to sing for Van Halen again."

"Or Peter Gabriel coming back to replace an injured Phil Collins in Genesis," Teddy said.

"Who?" Nick asked.

"Never mind," Teddy answered with a shake of his head.

"Damn Special K, you are old," Joey laughed.

"So the show goes on. The band puts Diana's mom in the front row and that's where she met Diana's dad. Three years later, Diana and her parents are at the Milford train station waiting for the train to New York and Diana fell off the platform seconds before the train came through. Guess who else was there that morning?"

"Vanilla Ice," Joey offered.

"No. And that was a terrible guess," Nick answered. "I was there with my parents. Of course I don't remember being there because I was only three, but when Diana fell off the platform, my dad saw it and was the one to reach her. He saved her life. Fifteen years later, she and I met in college."

"Get the hell out," Joey said.

"Your dad saved your wife's life?" Teddy asked.

Nick nodded.

"That's incredible. I'm a big believer in destiny. If Betsy's father hadn't died, I obviously wouldn't have had to come back for the funeral and we wouldn't have been reunited. And if I hadn't run into Mr. Fujitsu's brother at the cemetery, I probably wouldn't have taken the principal's job at Bishop Martin."

"And if you hadn't taken that, who knows where I'd be right now?" Joey lamented.

"Probably fencing diamonds or selling illegal arms to Middle Eastern countries," Nick offered.

"Thanks, pal."

"No problem."

"I'm going to go check on Conner," Teddy said.

The women left the room when he entered to give him some time to himself. Conner's vitals were about the same and he was still asleep.

"Well, pal, I hope you're fighting this with all your might," Teddy said, "because I don't know what your mother and I would do without you. I don't tell you as often as I should, but you're a great kid. You could do anything you want with your life. You could be a senator, president, a professor, run your own business. I don't really care what you do with your life as long as you live it well and enjoy it."

Teddy had never considered himself a religious man, save for being an alter boy when he was 12, but he had prayed more in recent weeks than he had in his entire life. Looking to the ceiling, he tried again.

"Please God, give him a chance. A chance to live the life I know he will. One that helps people. Because that's the kind of kid he is. Just give him that chance. Not for me. Or even for Betsy. But because I know Conner is special and he will make you proud."

God didn't respond right away. In fact, he didn't respond for nearly five days, but when he did, it was obvious he had listened. Teddy was asleep in the chair next to Conner's bed, much the way he had been for the past four nights. His hand covered his eyes to block out the sunlight that was creeping into the room, and he was hunched over in a not very comfortable looking position. But when you haven't slept in a week, nearly any position would suffice.

"I'm hungry," the voice in the bed declared.

Thinking he was still dreaming, Teddy didn't open his eyes at first.

"Dad, I'm hungry," the voice declared again.

Teddy slowly slid his hand down his face and looked up into his son's open blue eyes. "Pal. You're awake," he said before yelling into the other room, "He's awake! Everyone get in here! He's awake!!!"

Betsy, Nick, Diana and Joey raced each other into the room, but there was no way anyone was beating Betsy in that race.

"How do you feel?" Teddy asked hopefully.

"I feel ok," Conner responded as he started to sit up.

"Ok like better than you've been feeling? Or ok like ok?"

"Ok like ok," he answered. "I'm hungry."

"What would you like?" Betsy asked, tears streaming down her face.

"I'd like chili."

"Why don't we start with some toast and then go from there?" Teddy said. "Let's get this man some toast!"

They all ran from the room as if making toast was a five person job.

"And dad?"

Teddy stopped in the doorway. "Yeah, pal?"

"Don't worry. I promise I'll live a good life and make you proud."

He could feel a lump in his throat and his tear ducts filling simultaneously. "I know you will, pal. I know you will."

XXVII   FINAL DESTINARE

Two days after he woke up, Conner Kerrigan walked into the doctor's office for blood work. He looked like any other healthy nine year old boy. Fidgety. Bouncing off the walls. Talkative. They rushed the results through and when his doctor called the following morning, you could hear the shock in his voice.

"I don't understand this at all," the doctor said. "But there is barely a trace of cancer in his bloodstream. If he hadn't been so sick for so long, I would think there was a mistake in the previous blood work."

"You didn't make a mistake," Betsy said. "He was cured."

"I don't understand."

She then went on to explain what had happened to the astonished doctor. That same morning, high ranking officials in the Federal Drug Administration were arrested on charges of Obstructing Justice, Sharing Confidential Information and Conspiracy to Commit Murder. The drug company Cache was shut down. The person who had ordered the hit on Diana Moretti wasn't available for prison since he had rather inconveniently died of a stroke, but those that were next in command had received the message loud and clear. Two of them were also indicted on charges.

For Nick Moretti, the time had come to research something that had long been on his mind. Something that was further triggered by his conversation with Teddy a few nights earlier. He scoured the internet for signs of Philip Halmer. Articles. Address. Obituary. Nick's mother had said she lost contact with him years ago after Nick's father had died. Finally, he found a David Halmer in the town where Phil had last lived. He was hoping he was a relative.

"I'm trying to reach Phil Halmer please," he said to the person that answered on the other end of the line. "My father, who has since passed away, used to be very good friends with him."

"Who was your father?" asked the steely voice.

"Joe Moretti."

"Your father was a good man, and a good friend to my brother," the voice said, softening now. "I was sorry to hear he had passed."

"Thank you. Is there a way I could reach Phil?" Nick asked hopefully.

"I wish there was, but Phil passed away before your dad did. Phil died more than 30 years ago."

There was silence on the other end of the phone.

"Hello?" Phil's brother asked, checking to see if Nick was still on the line.

"Yes. I'm...I'm sorry. I had no idea," Nick answered.

As soon as he hung up, he Googled the band, *Running Water.* What he found was, "Running Water was a multi-platinum selling rock band in the 70's and early 80's. Frontman Adam Harper led the band from its inception in 1975 through 1980, and again in 1986 for a single reunion concert when his replacement was injured in a bus accident on the way to the show."

He then Googled Adam Harper and found, "Following a reunion show with the band in 1986, Harper was never heard from or seen in public again."

His wife was packing up the car in the driveway for the return trip home when he came outside.

"There's somewhere I need to stop quickly before we leave town," Nick said.

They had driven about five minutes before turning into the Fairfield High School parking lot.

"Who do you have to see here?" Diana asked.

"I'll explain on the drive home," Nick answered as he jumped from the car. "I'll be back in a few minutes."

Nick was buzzed into the front office and asked the smiling lady behind the counter, "I was wondering if you could page Tim Fujitsu down to the office in between periods? I was a friend of his brother and happened to be in town. Wanted to say a quick hello."

Nick grabbed a seat in one of the uncomfortable chairs in the office and waited for about ten minutes before the bell rang, sounding the end of the period. He heard the announcement paging Tim and moments later, he appeared. Tim and his brother were separated in age by three years, but could have passed as twins. Nick rose and extended a hand.

"Mr. Fujitsu. I'm Nick Moretti. I had your brother as a teacher at Bishop Martin."

"Of course, Nick. I remember you. Chuck always spoke highly of you. What can I do for you?"

"Well, this is going to sound like a strange question, but I was wondering if you remember going to Jim Holt's funeral about ten years ago?"

"I actually wasn't there," Tim answered. "I would have definitely gone if I was in town, but my son was studying abroad and I was visiting him in Spain at the time I heard. I remember feeling badly for not being able to attend. Why do you ask?"

"A friend said he ran into you at the funeral and that your conversation with him changed the course of his life."

"What friend?"

"Teddy Kerrigan."

"He's a good man. He's done a lot of good things at Bishop Martin. My brother would have been proud of him. But I didn't see him at Jim Holt's funeral. Must have been some other Asian guy," Tim laughed.

Nick walked slowly to the car where his wife was waiting not so patiently for him. She had a meeting at the FDA first thing in the morning and needed to prepare. She had lives to save.

But he had problems of his own to solve. What did Philip Halmer, Adam Harper and Chuck Fujitsu all have in common? Were they ghosts? Figments of people's imagination? Was destiny a matter of free will? Or was it free will with the occasional nudge in the right direction? Was each person a prop, an advocate or a driving force?

Nick came to the conclusion that it was all of the above. Every day, people made decisions that affected another person's life. Occasionally, those decisions seemed to be "guided" by some outside force. Then those people made decisions that affected another person... and another... and another... and another... until the circle was eventually completed and they all arrived at their destiny.

AUTHOR'S NOTES

Have you ever passed by someone you found attractive, but not had the courage to approach them? Have you in turn wondered if your life would have been different if you had? What if you missed someone by five minutes that could have altered the path of your existence? Or maybe arriving five minutes late saved your life? Are we driving our own destiny, or are there outside forces that influence our decisions and guide us along the road of discovery?

Destinare is a story of what ifs that shows how each decision we make has the ability to impact the lives of people in ways we could have never even imagined.

I am the master of my fate. I am the captain of my soul.

Originally written by the poet William Ernest Henley in *Invictus*, it was later altered slightly by Winston Churchill in his speech to the House of Commons in 1941 when he said, "We are still masters of our fate. We are still captain of our souls."

But are we?

Enjoy this book? Turn the page for a look at the opening chapter of another Micros novel, The Music Box...

The knock on the door came early, the way most bad news did. Jane Reynolds' ex-husband was dying and had one final wish—to spend his remaining days with his 12 year old son. On their way to visit him, and at her son's urging, Jane stops at a seedy pawn shop in an even seedier part of town, so Josh can buy a music box for his father. What he doesn't realize is that every song it plays, has the ability to transport both father and son back to the time his father first heard it.

Through his visits, Josh begins to finally see who his father really is, as well as learn some valuable life lessons along the way. Is it the magic of the music box? The sway of the music itself? Or the sheer power of the human mind at work? The Music Box is a story about a father and son, but it is a story for everyone who believes in family and second chances.

I
JOSH~

Josh Reynolds had a perpetual smile on his face, even when he was nervous—which he was at that very moment. He was mid-to-late 30-something, but looked much younger than his age. Nearly always crisply dressed in a pressed, blue Oxford and khakis, on this day, his shirt was unbuttoned at the top and the sleeves folded up twice on each side. A tie hung loosely around his neck. That was Saturday casual dress at the biggest advertising agency in the world. He hated working weekends like most people hated the dentist, but deadlines were deadlines, and clients didn't differentiate between weekdays and weekends.

He checked his watch as he stepped into the elevator, before he realized he was stepping in front of a woman. He stopped, placed his arm in front of the doors, and waited for her to enter. She smiled at him the way all women did. Didn't matter who they were, women were drawn to his manners, easy charm and clean-cut good looks. They were gifts from his father without him even realizing it.

The door opened on the 2nd floor and

a disheveled looking man in his mid-20's stepped on. He looked as though he had been up most of the night. It was all he could do to nod at Josh in acknowledgment.

"Morning, Petey," Josh said. "You ready for the big presentation?"

"I think so," Pete answered with somewhat less confidence than Josh was hoping for.

"Well, let's hear it."

Pete paused, then motioned with his hands as if he was creating a billboard. "Why buy just one, when it might take five to do the trick?"

Josh stared at him in disbelief, his jaw dropping to almost floor level. "You're joking, right?"

"I don't think so," he said sheepishly.

"Petey, we're selling feminine protection here, not breath mints!"

"Well, we thought about going the other way. *Why buy a whole box, when one might do the trick?* But we thought the client might think we were encouraging people to buy less of their product."

"Good thinking," Josh said sarcastically. "Look, your saying will get people thinking about women who have..."

Pete looked puzzled. "Who have what?"

"Who have a heavy...you know."

"Heavy--"

The woman, silent until this point, leaned in. "Flow," she whispered.

"Thank you," Josh nodded before turning

back to Pete. "Petey, we need to fix this or Bill's going to have a shit right there in the conference room. I'm going to go stall him. You and Jimbo need to come up with an alternate slogan. And you need to do it fast, because my son's basketball game starts in two hours out in Connecticut."

"I think it might be a little late for that."

"Why??"

"Because Bill sent someone down to pick it up earlier this morning, so he could have an advance look

at it."

"And you gave it to him??!!"

"He's my boss," Pete explained.

"I'M your boss!"

"But he's your boss."

"Which is why you should let me deal with him! This is not good. Bill's going to toss us all out of the 11th floor conference room window."

The elevator doors opened, and Josh raced down the hall to Bill Palmer's office. As he approached it, he could already hear Bill yelling from inside.

"Find Josh Reynolds!" Bill screamed at his secretary.

Josh motioned to her to pretend she hadn't seen him and did an abrupt 180 degree turn in the hallway. She just smiled at him. The way all women did.

Five minutes later, Josh slid into a seat next to Pete and Jim in the back of the conference room. There were ten other executives also in attendance. This would not be a pleasant experience he concluded.

"Did he look at the ad?" Pete asked nervously.

"I think it's safe to say that he did."

"Did he like it?"

"Let's just say, I hope your resume is up to date."

Bill entered the room. He was in his early 50's, with a thick head of mostly dark hair, with some grey sprinkled in. He had started as a copywriter twenty-seven years ago and worked his way up to CEO, stopping for a brief time at every rung of the ladder along the way. He was loud, bombastic even, but it was difficult not to respect a man who had actually worked his way to the top instead of having it handed to him.

"Josh," Bill began surprisingly calmly.

"Yes, Bill."

"What are my feelings on hiring morons?"

"You're generally opposed to it," Josh responded matter-of-factly, as if he was stating company policy.

"Exactly. It makes for bad business."

"That makes sense."

"Glad you agree with me. Now explain to me then, knowing how I feel about this, why you would put two morons in charge of one of our most lucrative clients?"

"Poor judgment on my part?" Josh offered, sending a steely look Pete and Jim's way.

"And what do they call the person who hired

the two morons?" Bill continued.

"A bigger moron?"

"Exactly. *Why buy one when it might take five to do the trick??* Jesus H, we're not selling Hot Tamales here!"

Josh looked back at Pete as if to say he told him so.

"What's the single most important factor to consider when selling feminine products?" Bill asked. "Jean?"

Jean was in her late 40's, most likely past her tampon usage days. Her eyes grew wide. She wasn't expecting to have to answer any questions. She preferred to work behind the scenes and be neither praised nor yelled at.

"Comfort?" she responded shyly.

"Good. And what else? Josh?"

"Uh, I've never used one, Bill."

"Neither have I," he answered, not missing a beat. "But I've seen them in trashcans. I'm sure you have too. And what's your reaction when you stumble onto one?"

"Eww?"

"Exactly. And what is one of the primary advantages our product offers?"

"Discretion?"

"Bullseye. So let's sell some goddamn discretion then! What I need is for you and the other two morons to sit here until you figure this shit out. Tell your wives you won't be home until you've got a slogan we can pitch. I've got to go see my chiropractor. Text me when you're done."

Josh rose from his seat. He knew it was a poor time to make a stand, but decided to make it anyway. "Bill," he said as he checked his watch, "I've actually got to leave for a while. My son's league championship basketball game starts in forty-five minutes out in Connecticut."

"And I'm sure it will be a helluva game. But he's ten."

"12 actually."

"Fine. He's 12. But don't act like it's the NBA Finals. Take care of this, Josh, because the only thing worse than being the guy who hired two morons is being the guy who hired the moron who hired two morons. Because you know what that makes him?"

"The biggest moron?"

"Exactly. And I have no intention of being the biggest moron."

"I hear ya, Bill. But I still have to leave."

There was a palatable uncomfortableness in the room.

"I wouldn't if you value your job."

"I do. Value my job that is. But I value my son even more. I'll make sure I'm reachable and will stay up all night if I need to, in order to make this right," Josh said as he made his way toward the door, leaving a stunned Bill in his wake. He decided not to look back because he knew if he did, he might start to have second thoughts.

Josh made what was usually a 50 minute drive in 39 minutes and slid into a seat in the bleachers next to a pretty blonde woman a few years younger than him.

Colleen Reynolds was the soccer mom who brought the oranges at halftime of games. The mother that all teenage boys eventually got teased about because she was so attractive. The wife that made Josh the envy of all his friends, and even a few enemies. Colleen was a sweetheart, but like all good mothers, someone who was fiercely protective of her son.

"Didn't think you were going to make it," she said.

"Yeah, I had to walk out in the middle of a meeting and drive 120 miles an hour on the Merritt in order *to* get here, but I wouldn't have missed it."

"He's been looking into the stands every couple of minutes for you."

Almost on cue, Timmy Reynolds looked up, broke into a wide smile and waved to his father. It suddenly made the nerve-wracking drive and his job uncertainty completely worthwhile.

"Little boys and their fathers," Colleen smiled. "He lights up every time you walk into a room."

"Give it a couple of years and he'll be giving me the finger and telling me I'm an a-hole," Josh answered. "By the way, I hope you're well-stocked in feminine products, because I don't think we're going to be getting any more free samples any time soon."

Thirty-two text messages and four phone calls from Pete later, and they finally had a new slogan.

He missed a few minutes of the game, but at least he was there. Later that night, he entered his son's dimly lit room to tuck him in and sat down on one corner of the bed.

"Night, pal," Josh said. "You played a great game today."

"Thanks for comin, dad," Timmy answered, before adding what was really on his mind.

"You're not going to get fired, are you?"

"Of course not. Why do you ask?"

"Because mom said you left an important meeting to come to my game."

"I'll be ok. Besides, like my dad used to say, 'Family first, last, and in between,'" Josh said as he stood in the doorway. "Night, pal."

"What was he like?" Timmy asked.

"What was who like? My dad?" Josh responded, a bit surprised by the question.

It was something that had been on Timmy's mind for a while. His grandfather had passed away before he had been born, but since his dad rarely spoke of him, he hadn't before mustered the courage to ask.

"Yeah."

"He was..." Josh reflected, "Complicated. But he was a good man."

Josh nodded. He seemed pleased with himself that he had found the right word to describe him.

"Did he used to go to your games?"

"Yes. But I didn't know it at the time."

"How come?"

"It's kind of a long story, pal."

"I'm not very tired," Timmy reasoned.

Josh mulled it over.   Decided there was no time like the present. After a slight pause, he began, "My dad.....was smart. He was athletic. Funny. Charming. Beautiful women fell all over him."

"How do you know that?"

"He got your grandmother to marry him,

didn't he?"

"No offense, dad, but grandma's old—and wrinkly."

Josh chuckled, "Well, she wasn't always. When your grandmother was younger, everyone thought she was gorgeous."

"Tell me more about your dad," Timmy urged.

"I'll tell you about him on two conditions. One. You keep it between you and I. Not even your mother or grandmother know some of the things I'm about to tell you. And two. If your mother walks in, you shut your eyes and pretend to be asleep so she doesn't yell at me for keeping you up past your bedtime. Deal?"

"Deal," Timmy assured him as he sat up in bed waiting for the story to begin.

"Ok, then. It was my 12th birthday...."